THE HAUNTED FIRE

A LIN COFFIN COZY MYSTERY
BOOK 17

J. A. WHITING

Copyright 2023 J.A. Whiting and Whitemark Publishing

Cover copyright 2023 Signifer Book Design

Formatting by Signifer Book Design

Proofreading by Donna Rich (donnarich@me.com) and Riann Kohrs (www.riannkohrs.com)

This book is a work of fiction. Names, characters, places, or incidents are products of the author's imagination or are used fictitiously. Any resemblance to locales, actual events, or persons, living or dead, is entirely coincidental.

All rights reserved.

No part of this publication can be reproduced or transmitted in any form or by any means, electronic or mechanical, without permission in writing from J. A. Whiting.

To hear about new books and book sales, please sign up for my mailing list at:
jawhiting.com

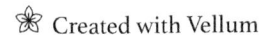

❀ Created with Vellum

Use your magic for good

1

The morning sun peered through the branches of the ancient oak tree, casting dappled light on Lin Coffin's face. A landscaper with an unusual gift, she paused to take in the beauty of her island home. Nantucket held a special place in her heart not only for its cozy, picturesque atmosphere and charm, but also for the connection it provided to her ancestors who had passed down their ability to see ghosts.

Lin's long brown hair blew gently in the breeze as she stood there, blue eyes surveying the work ahead. She and her business partner and friend, Leonard Reed, were about to tackle another day of heavy work transforming the property of their newest client.

"Morning, Coffin," Leonard called, emerging

from his pickup truck with a tool belt slung over his shoulder. He was a tall man in his sixties with muscular shoulders and arms that spoke of decades spent working outdoors. Despite his age, he moved with ease, a testament to his years of keeping fit.

"Morning, Leonard," Lin replied, offering a warm smile. There was something particularly comforting about Leonard's presence in her life. Not only was he a dear friend, but he also understood her unique gift without judgment or fear.

When Lin arrived back on Nantucket after spending years away on the mainland going to college and working, she met and interacted with Leonard. She'd believed the man had murdered someone, and when she realized her mistake, she was terribly ashamed of assuming he was the killer.

A few years ago, Lin approached him about starting their own landscaping business, and together, they'd built a well-respected landscaping company known for its beautiful and innovative designs. From manicured lawns to lush gardens, their work was in demand all over the island.

Lin's small brown rescue dog Nicky ran to greet the man, and Leonard bent to pat the happy animal. "How's it going, Nick? Ready for the day?" The dog squirmed and practically smiled up at him.

The hinges of the garden gate creaked open as Lin entered the sideyard. Tall privet hedges lined the path, their gnarled branches intertwining overhead to form a leafy tunnel. She sighed, running a gloved hand over the hedge's rough surface. She'd never gotten used to the lingering scent of privet— a tiny bit of sweet combined with musty and bitter, like old books left in an attic.

As they set about their tasks, Lin found herself lost in thought. Something had been picking at her from the moment she'd woken up that morning, but she couldn't figure out what was bothering her.

"Everything okay?" Leonard asked, seeing her faraway expression.

"Fine, just thinking about this project," she fibbed, forcing her thoughts back to the task at hand.

"All right," Leonard said, accepting her answer without pressing further. He knew when to give Lin space, and she was grateful for that. "Quite the maze, isn't it?"

A faint smile tugged at Lin's lips. After several years as business partners, she still loved working on every new project they did together. "It's going to be fun turning this mess of a yard into an English country garden."

Leonard snorted, running his hand through his

hair. "I'm not sure about fun. It better end up being perfect. The owners want it to look like something out of a picture book, all manicured lawns, rosebushes, and wildflowers."

"Well, the check cleared, so they're the boss," Lin kidded as she began walking into the rear yard with Leonard falling into step beside her.

Looking around the space, the man shrugged. What seemed simple on paper often proved far more complicated in reality. "At least the privet's healthy," Leonard said, eyeing the dense foliage. "We'll have our work cut out for us clearing space for those rosebushes, though."

Lin sighed, bracing herself for the strenuous work to come. Long hours of digging, planting, and pruning stretched ahead, but she wouldn't trade her job for anything. Nantucket was her home, and bringing beauty to its yards and gardens was what she loved to do. Even the ghosts that often drifted through and needed so much of her attention couldn't dampen her love for the place. Over time, Lin had grown more comfortable with her gift and the ghosts that appeared to her often seemed like old friends. Through the years, she'd learned to interpret the spirits' silent gestures and cryptic messages using her unique connection to help those who had unfinished business on the earthly plane.

Her ability to see ghosts was just another aspect of who she was, as familiar now as the scent of turned earth or the weight of pruning shears in her hands. After so many years, she often knew how to interpret the clues the spirits left behind; a strange chill, the faint scent of lilies that only she could smell, a flicker at the edge of her vision. The ghosts of Nantucket were woven into the fabric of the island, as much a part of her home as the beaches, dune grass, and antique houses.

∽

When the workday was done and after taking a hot shower at home, Lin left her cozy house and walked along the brick sidewalks heading into town. She breathed in a long breath of the salt air. Even in spring and early summer, there could be a chill to the breeze off the harbor.

At the top of Main Street, a flash of movement caught her eye. A man stood under the branches of an oak tree, dressed in a grey overcoat and wearing a cap. As Lin watched, he turned his head to stare directly at her, his eyes glinting from under the brim of his hat. The man's atoms shimmered; he was nearly see-through. From the pallor of his skin and the way he seemed slightly out of focus as if glimpsed through a veil, she knew right away what she was seeing.

Her breath caught in her throat and her heart pounded.

A ghost.

Lin didn't say anything; she just kept her eyes on his. She sensed the spirit's gentle manner, honesty, and kindness. She was never afraid when a ghost appeared to her; she knew he or she had come to her for help, and Lin was always determined to do what she could for them.

In a few moments, the ghost's atoms sparkled and swirled faster and faster until they sparked, and in an instant, he was gone.

Lin let out a long breath. *What do you need, my friend?* she wondered silently, staring at the spot on the sidewalk where the ghost had stood.

Giving herself a little shake, she continued into town, her head filled with questions about the new ghost. She walked until she reached her cousin's popular bookstore and café, Viv's Victus. The shop was located on the cobblestone main street of the town's center. The place was always busy with customers browsing the book aisles and sitting at the café tables sipping beverages and eating cake, soup, or sandwiches. Stepping inside, the cheerful jingle of the doorbell welcomed her.

Lin headed for the back of the store to the café section. Viv glanced up from the counter where she was restocking pastries, and her brow furrowed.

"What's the matter with you? What's wrong?" Viv was a short pretty young woman, and she and Lin were cousins who shared the same birthday. Viv had lived on Nantucket all of her life except for her four years away at college and a summer spent in Europe traveling with a choral group.

The cousins were descended from two different lines of the Coffin family on their fathers' sides, but their mothers had been sisters whose ancestors were from the Witchard family of Nantucket. Viv carried a few extra pounds and had chin-length light brown hair flecked with gold that was cut in layers around her face. She had lovely skin, rosy cheeks, and a warm, friendly smile.

Lin bit her lip, hesitating. Viv had known about her cousin's ability for ages and always helped her with the spirits. Occasionally, Viv, too, could see the ghosts, but it wasn't a skill she wanted or cultivated.

"I saw something ... at the top of Main Street," Lin told Viv.

"Like what?" Viv came out from behind the counter and then stopped short and stared, realizing what her cousin meant. "Oh." She took Lin's arm and steered her to one of the café tables where they both took seats. "Tell me."

Lin looked down at the tabletop for a moment, trying to collect her thoughts and recall what she'd sensed when the ghost appeared. "It was a middle-aged man. He was standing on the sidewalk. He was dressed as if he were from the early 1900s. He made eye contact with me. I got the feeling he was a good person."

Viv waited for Lin to go on.

"We only looked at one another for a few seconds, and then he was gone." Lin closed her eyes and took in a long breath before opening them again. "I felt ... loss. I felt a sadness and grief coming from him. He wants my help, but I have no idea with what."

Viv touched her cousin's hand. "You'll figure it out. You always do."

"No matter how many times I see a new ghost..." Lin kept her voice soft. "...I worry I might not be able to help them." Sitting with her cousin in the cozy warmth of Viv's bookstore, Lin's mind continued to whirl with thoughts of the ghost she'd encountered. She couldn't verbally communicate with the spirits, but her experiences had taught her that paying close attention to when and where they appeared, along with their reactions to her, could provide vital clues about their intentions.

"We'd better get going." Lin stood. "We don't want to be late." Their friends Libby Hartnett and Anton Wilson had invited the cousins to meet for dinner down by the docks.

Leaving the bookshop, Lin and Viv strolled together along the narrow streets of Nantucket. The sun had dipped close to the horizon and shadows were creeping across the cobblestone streets. The picturesque scenery took on a darker tone and Lin felt a shiver run down her spine. As she glanced around at the familiar sights, her thoughts drifted to the spirits that lingered just out of sight and wondered where the new ghost was about to lead her.

2

The setting sun cast an orange glow over Nantucket Harbor as Lin and Viv approached the quaint, seaside restaurant. The harbor was bustling with activity, and tourists and townsfolk filled the sidewalks.

There was an underlying sense of tension in the salty air which caused Viv to fiddle nervously with the clasp on her purse. "Do you feel that?" she asked hesitantly, her eyes searching Lin's face for any sign of agreement.

"I do. Something seems off, but I don't know why. You're feeling it, too?" Lin asked, her blue eyes narrowing as she scanned the crowd for any signs of the ghost she saw earlier.

"Maybe it's just the humidity." Viv's cheeks were

flushed. "Let's enjoy our dinner with Libby and Anton. We can focus on weird feelings later."

As they entered the cozy dining area, the two women spotted their companions sitting at a window-side table with a view of the harbor. Libby Hartnett, a lifelong resident of Nantucket and a distant cousin of Lin's, had strong paranormal powers and had been a mentor to the young woman, helping her to accept her ability to see ghosts. Unsure of Libby's age, Lin and Viv guessed she might be in her early eighties. She was an active, pretty woman with mesmerizing blue eyes and silvery white hair layered around her face.

Beside Libby sat Anton Wilson. In his seventies, he was an island historian and expert on Nantucket's past, an author, and former history professor. The man often assisted Lin by researching the spirits she encountered.

While Anton peered at the menu and Libby chatted with the waitress, Lin waved to get their attention.

"Ah, there you are," Libby exclaimed, gesturing them over. Her eyes sparkled as she welcomed the cousins to the table. "Come, sit down."

"Good evening, you two," Anton greeted them,

pushing his black-framed eyeglasses up to the bridge of his nose and giving the cousins a warm smile.

Lin and Viv took seats after giving Libby and Anton quick hugs.

"You're both looking well," Libby said with a smile, her wise eyes crinkling at the corners. "What's new?"

"We have new clients," Lin said, excitement flashing across her features. "Leonard and I met with a nice couple recently who want us to transform their two-acre property into an English garden. It's going to be quite a challenge, but we're looking forward to it. We just got started this morning."

"Sounds wonderful," Libby mused, sipping her wine. "How was your day at the bookstore, Vivian?"

"Busy as always," Viv replied with a smile. "The shop was packed today. The tourists can't get enough of our local history books and Nantucket-themed gifts."

Anton set down the menu. "How was the book signing the other day?"

"It went really well." Viv tucked a stray lock of hair behind her ear. "The new paranormal mystery sold out." She launched into an exciting recap of the event, describing the line of customers wrapping around the block and the intimate Q&A session with the author.

Lin stifled a chuckle, exchanging a glance with Libby. If only the customers knew how much first-hand experience they all had with the paranormal. She mentally shook off the thought, not wanting to dwell on the ghostly figure she'd seen earlier that day. There would be time enough to discuss it over dinner. She picked up her menu, the corners of her mouth turning up into a smile. It was good to spend time with friends who understood her in a way most others never could.

They placed their orders and chatted casually until the food arrived. When Lin took a sip of her wine, Libby stared at her with narrowed eyes. "Is something going on?"

With a sigh, Lin marveled at how the woman picked up on every little thing. "I saw something today at the top of Main Street."

Anton's eyes widened as he kept his voice down. "A ghost?"

Lin nodded, glancing out the window where the previous orange glow in the sky had deepened into darkness. The tension she'd felt earlier still lingered, sending a shiver over her skin.

Libby set down her glass, concern etched into her features. "Tell us about the ghost, dear."

Lin described the figure in as much detail as possible: the old-fashioned clothes, the somber expression, the deep sense of loss that had emanated from its translucent form. "It's clear this spirit is deeply troubled. He gives off a terrible sense of loss and grief." She trailed off for a moment, her eyebrows knitting together. "The ghost is mourning something—or someone. He also seems to be fearful of something. If we can discover what or whom, maybe we can help him find peace."

"Do you think there's a connection between this ghost and the recent house fires on the island?" Anton questioned.

Lin's face went blank.

"Have you heard about the house fires, Carolin?" Libby's expression was serious.

"There have been two so far," Anton replied solemnly. "All in old homes with historic significance. It's quite concerning."

Viv said, "Yeah, we heard about them."

Lin blinked. "The authorities were investigating the blazes. Weren't they just electrical issues? What could that have to do with the new spirit?"

Anton's gaze was sharp behind the lenses of his glasses. "They were arson ... both of them."

Lin's throat tightened. "Has the person who set the fires been caught?"

"No. It's an ongoing investigation." Libby glanced out the window, and then she turned back to Lin. "The new ghost might have a link to these fires?"

"I can't say for sure. I've only seen him once, and only for a few moments." Lin shook her head. "But it seems too coincidental to be unrelated. This ghost is mourning something and I have no idea what."

Libby asked, "And you're certain this spirit means no harm?"

"Positive." Lin smiled weakly. "He wants help. He needs someone to understand his plight."

Anton nodded. "I'll be happy to help out with any needed research."

"And I'll help you any way I can," Libby added. "You're not alone in this, Carolin." The woman turned her gaze to the flickering candle on the table. "With your ability to see ghosts, perhaps you'll uncover something the local authorities haven't."

Viv smiled at her cousin. "The ghost has come to the right person for help."

Lin felt a rush of gratitude for her friends and their support. With their help, she hoped to solve the mystery of this gentle spirit. She took another sip of wine, determination settling into her bones.

When dinner had come to an end and the dessert plates had been whisked away by the cheerful waitress, Lin took a sip of her coffee. The bitterness mingled with the sweet taste of tiramisu still lingering on her tongue. The restaurant's dim lighting cast shadows on the walls, and Lin felt that it matched the atmosphere of her day. She took a deep breath, feeling the weight of responsibility settle on her shoulders. The ghost's profound grief haunted her, tugging at her heartstrings. She would never walk away from someone in need – living or dead.

As they left the restaurant, Lin felt tension in her neck as if the shadows were watching her every move.

The streetlamps cast their lovely light on the cobblestone streets as the cousins walked to Viv's house. Lin had left a sweater there a few days ago and was going to pick it up before heading to her own house. The two chatted amiably, but Lin couldn't shake off her unease about the ghost she'd seen earlier that day.

"Are you all right?" Viv asked.

"Still thinking about the ghost," Lin admitted, rubbing her arms to stave off the chill.

"Hopefully, we'll find some answers soon," Viv reassured her, giving her cousin a gentle pat on the back.

They walked a few more blocks in comfortable silence, but as they turned onto Viv's street, an acrid smell drifted on the air.

Smoke.

Hurrying down the lane, they saw it. Flames shot through the windows of a house, painting the night sky with vivid hues of orange and red. Thick black smoke billowed from the roof, choking the air with its sharp scent.

"I'll call for help," Lin shouted as she fumbled for her phone. Her hands trembled, and her heart pounded wildly as she and Viv hurried to the home's front door.

"Is anyone in there?" Viv yelled, pounding desperately on the door. No answer came, only the roar of the flames and the crackle of burning wood.

"911, what's your emergency?" the voice asked.

"House fire!" Lin gasped into the phone, struggling to keep her voice steady. "We need help!"

"Please give me the address," the operator instructed.

Lin choked out the words, her eyes watering at the thickening smoke. "I'm not sure if anyone's inside."

"Firefighters are on their way. Please stand back and wait for them to arrive."

"Got it," Lin said, disconnecting the call. "You didn't hear anyone inside?" she asked Viv, her voice straining with urgency.

"All I hear is the noise from the fire," Viv cried, her fear and frustration evident. "I don't know if anyone's in there." She rang the bell and pounded on the door one more time.

"Let's get back to the sidewalk," Lin insisted, grabbing Viv's arm. "We have to stay out of the way when help arrives."

As they retreated, Lin felt a pang of guilt. What if someone was trapped inside, unable to escape? She cast one last, desperate glance at the burning house, praying that the fire department would arrive soon.

Other people began to gather on the sidewalk, and Lin and Viv answered their questions.

Viv began to pace nervously on the walkway. "Where are they? What's taking the firefighters so long to get here?"

Even from their vantage point across the street, Lin could feel the heat of the blaze against her cheeks. The crackling sounds of wood being consumed by the flames filled the air, an unsettling noise that sent shivers along her skin.

At last, the wail of sirens could be heard, announcing the arrival of the firetrucks. As they pulled up to the scene, the firefighters leapt into action, unraveling hoses and connecting them to the hydrant.

"Stay back," one of them warned the onlookers, ushering them further back from the heat and smoke.

The cousins watched helplessly as the firefighters battled the blaze, their hearts pounding with fear and concern for the residents who might be trapped inside. It felt like an eternity before they finally saw a figure being carried out of the smoke-filled doorway, limp and unconscious.

As they watched the ambulance speed away, sirens blaring, they hoped the neighbor would pull through.

The terrible scent of smoke still moved in the air as Lin and Viv stood watching the firefighters continue to battle the blaze. The once-peaceful night had turned into a chaotic whirlwind, filled with the frantic shouts of first responders and the concerned voices of neighbors.

"Excuse me." A firefighter approached, his helmet tucked under his arm. "Oh, Viv, Lin. You're the ones who called in the fire?"

"Hi, Michael," Viv said. "We were the first ones on the scene." Michael Hansson, a friend of Viv's husband, John, had been a Nantucket firefighter for many years.

Lin asked anxiously, "Is everyone all right?"

Michael hesitated for a moment, his expression somber. "The resident was found unconscious from smoke inhalation, but they were able to get him out in time. He's on his way to the hospital now."

"Thank goodness," Viv murmured, tears welling up in her eyes. "I just ... I can't believe this happened."

"Neither can I," Lin whispered, her voice barely audible as she clutched Viv's hand in a tight grip. Her gaze drifted toward the burning house.

The firefighter took a quick look at the home, and then turned back to the young women. "I already have your contact information. Someone from the department will be calling you in a day or two to talk about what you saw." He turned to head back to one of the trucks. "Stay safe," he advised before returning to his duties. Lin and Viv exchanged worried glances, the gravity of the situation sinking in.

"Michael is a good guy," Viv said and then sighed. "He's going through a rough patch. His wife left him a couple of months ago. They're separated. She left Nantucket and went back to the mainland with their two kids. I feel bad for him."

"That must be really tough. Let's go home," she suggested gently, and Viv nodded, too shaken to say anything more.

As they began to walk away, Lin suddenly felt a prickling sensation at the back of her neck. She glanced around, searching for the source of her unease ... and there, standing on the edge of the sidewalk, was the ghost from earlier in the day.

"Viv," Lin whispered, unable to tear her eyes away from the ghost. "Do you see that?"

"See what?" Viv asked, confusion on her face.

Lin's voice trembled as she tugged on her cousin's arm. "It's him, the ghost. He's here." She could feel the spirit's eyes on her, a silent plea for help radiating from its ethereal form.

"Where?" Viv asked, trying to follow Lin's gaze.

"Right there," she whispered, pointing at the spectral figure, but as Viv looked, the ghost sparkled and vanished, leaving only the flickering flames in his wake.

"He's gone." Lin's thoughts swirled with questions. What did this ghost want? And why had he appeared again now, at the fire? Was there a connection?

Lin glanced back at the burning building and then at the spot where the ghost had been standing. It was clear the spirit needed her help with something, but she didn't yet know what it was. What she did know, however, was that the ghost was not responsible for the fire – she sensed he was a good person, weighed down by grief and loss.

"I'll help you," Lin whispered into the night. "I promise."

With heavy hearts, the cousins walked away, the ghost's haunting gaze lingering in Lin's mind like an echo from long ago.

3
―――

Lin stood by the window, peering out into the foggy Nantucket night. The faint glow of distant streetlights cast shadows over the quiet lane. She shivered involuntarily as she recalled her recent encounter with the ghost – a man from another era who seemed to be connected to the mysterious house fires that had been plaguing the community. She saw her husband's truck pull into the driveway, and she and Nicky went to the front door to meet him.

They sat together at the kitchen table with cups of coffee while Jeff told her about his day working on an antique Cape-style house in 'Sconset. "How was your day? You and Viv met Libby and Anton for dinner?"

"We did. It was a nice time together." Lin took a

deep breath and hesitated for a moment, trying to find the right words. "When I was on my way to Viv's bookshop, I saw a ghost at the top of Main Street."

"A new one?" Jeff's eyebrows shot up, though his tone remained steady. "Things have been quiet recently. I wondered when a spirit might show up needing your help."

Lin swallowed hard, feeling a knot form in her stomach. "He's a middle-aged man dressed like he's from either the late 1800s or the early 1900s. He seems ... so sad like he carries a heavy worry or burden."

"Is the ghost angry?" Jeff had been in contact with an angry ghost once when Lin was trying to help a spirit, and he had to admit that being around the apparition had been an alarming experience.

"He isn't angry. He seems to be a gentle soul."

Nicky wagged his tail in agreement, headed to his dog bed where he circled a couple of times before settling, and then quickly dozed off.

"Do you think the ghost might be connected to the recent house fires?" Jeff asked, his voice laced with curiosity.

"I think he might be," Lin replied. "I have this gut feeling that if I can help him, maybe we can stop the arsonist before anyone gets seriously hurt."

Jeff nodded, reaching over to take her hand. His touch was warm and reassuring. "I'll do whatever it takes to help you help him. Just let me know if there's anything I can do."

"That means a lot to me." Lin took a sip of her coffee, feeling the warmth spread through her body as she contemplated her next move.

"Let's think about this logically," Jeff suggested. "If the ghost is connected to these recent events on the island, there must be some kind of link between his time and ours. You'll need to find out who he was and what happened to him."

"Right," Lin agreed, her determination increasing. "I have to think about where to start. We know so little about him, and ... well, it's not like we can just walk up to people and ask if they've seen any ghosts lately." She smiled.

"Definitely not," Jeff replied, a thoughtful expression crossing his face. "It seems like a trip to the historical society with Viv is needed to look into the history of island fires. There might be something in the old records that could shed light on the mystery, and if you get lucky, maybe you'll find a connection to the recent fires, too."

"I thought that would be the best way to start," Lin said, the weight on her chest beginning to lighten. "I can also ask Anton to look into house fires from the past, maybe narrowing it down to fires where people lost their lives."

Lin furrowed her brow as she and Jeff sat in the dimly lit kitchen, their hands wrapped around their warm mugs of coffee. "So there have been three house fires on the island so far this month," she began, her voice low and controlled. "The first one happened a little less than a month ago, the second was just last week, and then there's the fire at the house in Viv's neighborhood. It's way too much of a coincidence for them not to be connected. The authorities have determined the first two fires were arson."

Jeff nodded, his eyes reflecting the flicker of the candles in the middle of the table. "The most recent fire will probably be arson as well. It's certainly suspicious, and the fact that you started seeing the ghost around the time of the fires … there might be some connection there."

"Exactly," Lin whispered, her gaze drifting toward the window where the moon cast a silvery light over the garden outside. "That's why I think Viv and I should visit the houses that were set on fire. Maybe being there and seeing the aftermath will help us understand what's going on. We won't be able to enter the premises, but we might be able to walk around the properties."

"Good idea," Jeff agreed, his hand reaching out to give hers a reassuring squeeze. "Talk to Viv and figure out when you can go. Take Nicky along, too. He's proven to be very perceptive when it comes to these kinds of things."

Lin smiled softly at the mention of their rescue dog who was currently curled up on his bed by the door to the deck, his chest rising and falling rhythmically as he slept. She appreciated the comfort his presence brought, especially when there were ghosts to deal with. The dog always seemed to have a comforting effect on the spirits.

∼

It was early evening when Lin, Viv, and Nicky set out for the Cliff neighborhood to visit one of the houses that had been set ablaze. The air was tinged with a salty breeze as they drove along the narrow island roads. Their windows were rolled down to let in the fresh scent of the sea.

As they approached the house, Lin's heart dropped at the sight of the charred remains. Blackened timbers jutted out like skeletal fingers reaching for the sky, and the smell of smoke still hung heavy in the air. They parked the car and stepped out, Nicky bounding alongside them with his tail wagging energetically despite the somber scene.

When Lin's hand reached for the horseshoe necklace she was wearing, her fingers closed around the pendant. Her necklace was once owned by her ancestor Emily Witchard Coffin and was found in the attached storage shed of Viv's house, hidden there hundreds of years ago by Emily's husband Sebastian, an early settler of Nantucket.

The white-gold horseshoe was set in the center of the pendant and it tilted slightly to one side. The horseshoe design could be seen in the chimney bricks of several old houses on the island and was intended to ward off witches and evil spells, but Sebastian and Emily Coffin used the symbol on their own chimney to draw people who had been accused of witchcraft to their home to provide them with a safe place to stay as they settled on the island. Viv had given Emily Coffin's horseshoe necklace to Lin because Lin and Emily shared the same skill; both could see ghosts.

"Let's walk around the property," Lin suggested, her voice hushed as if speaking too loudly might disturb some unseen presence. "Maybe we can pick up on something, some clue as to why these fires were set."

"Sounds good," Viv agreed, her eyes scanning the wreckage. "I'll keep an eye out for anything that could help us understand what happened and why."

As they circled the remains of the house, Lin tried to focus on the task at hand, but she was distracted by the feeling that someone – or something – was watching them. She glanced over at Nicky who seemed to be picking up on her unease. His ears perked up and his gaze darted around in search of the source.

"Find anything?" Lin asked her cousin as they met back at the front of the house.

"Nothing concrete. It was a long shot," she admitted, frustration evident in her voice, "but I have a feeling that whoever is doing this has a heavy heart."

"You're picking up on that?" Lin was surprised at Viv. Her cousin had powers of her own but was frightened by them and usually didn't allow her skills to surface, preferring to let Lin handle the paranormal stuff.

Viv shrugged. "I tried not to sense anything, but the feeling is too powerful to ignore. I think the arsonist is dealing with some serious emotions ...

grief, anger, resentment. I can't put my finger on the specifics."

"Do you get any sense of the arsonist? A man? Woman? Age?"

"Not yet." Viv's eyes wandered over the charred remains of the large house.

"Does that mean you're going to allow your powers to come to the fore?"

"I want to help," Viv admitted. "My neighbor almost died. Libby's always telling me to use all of my skills. I'm going to take baby steps."

Lin gave her cousin's arm an affectionate squeeze. "I'm so glad. I need all the help I can get."

They left the Cliff neighborhood and headed for Orange Street. The moment they stepped foot on the sidewalk in front of the second damaged house, and despite the sun's warmth, Lin felt a sudden chill. She glanced at Nicky who had stopped in his tracks with his eyes fixated on something – or someone – that only he and Lin could see.

"Viv," Lin whispered, her voice barely audible. "He's here, the ghost."

"Where?" Viv asked with a nervous tone, concern furrowing her brow as she scanned the area around the Orange Street house, not wanting to see what Lin was seeing.

"By the tree near the edge of the property." Lin pointed, her eyes never leaving the figure of the middle-aged man from the late 1800s or early 1900s. He stood with a forlorn expression, looking at the burnt remains of the house. There was a kindness in his eyes that made Lin certain he wasn't responsible for the fires.

With his tail wagging, Nicky trotted over to the ghost, sat down on the grass, and stared up at the man. The ghost looked down at the animal and smiled.

"Can you ask him if he knows anything about the fires? Or how he's connected to them?" Viv prompted, fueled by her own curiosity.

"You know they really can't converse with me, but who knows? Maybe this spirit is different." Lin hesitated for a moment, then mustered her courage and approached the ghost. "Hello. I'm Lin Coffin, and that's my cousin Viv," she said softly, trying not to startle him. "I think you might need my help with something. I'll do my best to help you. We're also trying to find out more about the fires that have been set on the island. Is there any way you can tell me something about them? Or help me understand what it is you need?"

The ghost gave a hint of a head shake.

"Is your story somehow intertwined with these terrible events?"

The ghost held her eyes.

"Is there something specific that ties you to these fires?"

The ghost's face looked like it might crumble into tears as he looked away, and when the spirit finally returned his gaze to Lin, she felt a deep-seated grief and a sense that whatever was going on might span generations. The force of the feelings made her eyes shut briefly and she took a shaky step backwards.

Viv hurried to her cousin's side. "Are you all right? Did something happen? Is the ghost still here?"

Lin looked to the tree, but the spirit was gone.

"He disappeared." Lin shared the information with Viv, and they both stood in silence for a moment as they processed the ghost's feelings.

Finally, Viv spoke up. "Are we dealing with someone who has some sort of historical vendetta against the island?" She frowned. "That would really complicate things."

"I'm unsure. The ghost's feelings are strong, but they're not focused enough for me to understand them." Lin felt a cold chill run down her arms.

"Maybe it's a vendetta against specific families or people," Viv suggested, trying to make sense of it all. "There must be a reason why these particular houses were targeted."

"I know Anton is looking into the history of the families who lived in these houses to see if there's anything that might link the fires to certain people, but I think we should do some research into the ghost's own story, too." Lin let out a sigh. "This is going to be a very hard case."

"Agreed." Viv nodded. "Let's visit the burned house in my neighborhood later tonight. I walk past it multiple times a day, but I push down any feelings or sensations that might try to bubble up. I'll feel better if we try to pick up on things together."

Lin nodded. "And tomorrow we can go to the historical society. Maybe the historical record can help us untangle this mess."

Determination shined in Viv's eyes. "Tomorrow we'll find some answers."

They left the smoldering remains of the second house, their minds filled with unanswered questions.

4

It was late afternoon when the charred remains of David and Noelle Winchester's once beautiful home loomed before Lin and Viv, a stark reminder of the fire's devastating power. The smell of burnt wood and smoldering debris still lingered in the air. Lin scanned the wreckage, her athletic frame tense as she tried to make sense of what had happened.

"David is still in the hospital," Viv said of her sixty-six-year-old neighbor. She pushed her chin-length hair back from her face as she looked at Lin with concern.

"Yeah," Lin replied quietly, her eyes remaining fixed on the ruins. "His smoke inhalation was pretty serious, but they say he'll recover." She paused, swallowing hard as she fought back her emotions. "He's lucky to be alive."

Viv bit her lip, nodding slowly. "Poor David. He and his wife are such nice people. I'm glad Noelle wasn't at home at the time of the fire." Viv's warm, lovely smile was absent from her face, replaced by a look of worry. "So, what do we do now?"

Lin stared at the house for a moment longer, then turned to face her cousin. "We need to figure out who the ghost is and what connection he might have to these recent fires. Maybe then we can help the police uncover who did this and why. We can't let the arsonist get away with it."

"Oh, he won't," Viv said, her voice firm as she straightened her shoulders, ready to confront the challenges they faced.

Lin scanned the wreckage of Noelle and David's home, unable to shake off the heart-wrenching image of what had been lost. The scent of burnt wood and ash clung to her nostrils, each breath a sad reminder of the tragedy that had unfolded.

"David told his wife he wants to rebuild the house," Viv murmured.

Just then, a woman's voice called out to Viv, and she and Lin turned to see Noelle Winchester hurrying down the sidewalk toward them. "Hello there."

"Noelle." Viv gave the woman a long hug. "We're so sorry about the house. We were happy to hear that David will make a full recovery."

Lin offered sincere words as well.

"It's unbelievable." Noelle pushed a strand of her blonde hair over her ear. In her sixties, the woman was fit and trim and was a well-known fiber artist. "David might have some lingering breathing problems, but that should fade with time. Thank heavens he survived the fire. He'd been reading up in bed and fell asleep."

"Is there anything we can do to help out?" Lin asked.

"Thank you, but I don't think so. I'm staying with a friend until David gets out of the hospital." She turned to Viv. "In fact, this morning, I contacted your husband to find us a rental house to stay in for the summer."

"I'm sure John will find you what you need," Viv assured her neighbor.

Noelle's shoulders drooped a little. "David told me he saw a suspicious man hanging around before the fire started."

Lin's brain buzzed at the news. "A suspicious man?"

Noelle nodded. "He said he noticed a young man standing on the sidewalk staring at the house about an hour or so before he went up to read. He thought it odd but then brushed it off thinking the person must be a lover of historic houses."

"Did David describe the man?" Lin questioned.

"He told me he was slim and a little shorter than average height. He was wearing a baseball cap. It was dark outside at the time so David couldn't say anything more about the man's appearance." Noelle's face darkened. "The police are concerned that this is the third fire of suspicious origin this month. It makes me weak to think an arsonist deliberately set our house on fire."

After a few more minutes of conversation, Noelle said goodbye to the cousins and headed into town for a meeting.

"The arsonist must be responsible for this fire, too," Lin thought aloud, her mind racing as she considered the possibility. She looked at the blackened beams and partially collapsed roof. "But what could be the motive?"

Viv's eyes narrowed in thought. "I do think it was set on purpose, but it might have been a random choice. As far as motive, it's not unheard of for someone to start fires just for the thrill of it."

"Could someone have something against David or Noelle?" Lin clenched her fists, anger bubbling up inside her at the idea of someone intentionally causing so much pain and destruction.

"I doubt it. I really think it was random," Viv said, "unless the occupants of the houses have some link between them. But isn't that unlikely? Either way, we have to do more digging. There's an arsonist on the loose. We need to figure out what's going on. Who knows when he'll strike again?"

Lin nodded. "You're right. We owe it to David and to everyone else to figure this out," she said, her mind racing with ideas. "Maybe we can find a pattern that will lead us to the culprit."

Viv concurred. "Maybe John's friend in the police department can share some information that might help point us in the right direction."

"That's a great idea." Lin smiled, grateful for Viv's help and support. "Let's head to the historical society. Felix Harper has helped us in the past, and I'm sure he'll have some good insights about any historical fires that might be important."

"Sounds like a plan. Felix is always helpful," Viv replied as she fell into step beside Lin.

Together, they made their way into town to the historical society. As they approached the building, Lin felt a sudden chill run down her spine, causing her to shiver. She glanced around, searching for the source of the unsettling sensation, but there was nothing out of the ordinary and her ghost wasn't in sight.

"Lin?" Viv's voice pulled her cousin back from her thoughts. "Are you all right?"

"Y-yeah," Lin stammered, trying to shake off the uneasiness that had gripped her. "I just … I thought I felt something, but it's probably nothing."

"Well, when you feel something, it is never nothing," Viv said, still eyeing her cousin with worry. "Just let me know if anything seems off, okay? I prefer an early warning system. Don't let any ghosts sneak up on me."

Lin chuckled. "I won't," she agreed, though the lingering sense of unease continued to gnaw at her as they stepped inside the historical society. "At least, not if I can help it."

Viv used her elbow to give her cousin a poke.

∼

The scent of old books and polished wood welcomed Lin and Viv as they entered the historical society library. The late afternoon sunlight streamed through the tall windows and spilled across the worn floorboards. Lin's heart raced with anticipation as she looked about the room, searching for the familiar figure she knew could help them in their search for answers.

"Ah, there he is," Viv whispered, pointing toward a meticulously dressed man with his salt-and-pepper hair perfectly styled, carefully studying an old map spread out on a table before him.

Felix Harper looked up from his work, eyes brightening as he spotted the pair approaching. "Lin! Viv! What a pleasant surprise," he greeted them warmly, extending a hand to each of them. "What brings you to the museum today?"

"Hi, Felix," Lin said, exchanging a firm handshake with the stylish historian and librarian. "We were hoping you could help us with some research."

"Of course," Felix replied, his curiosity piqued. "What are you looking for?"

"Information on historical fires," Viv chimed in. "Specifically, any that might have been caused by arson from the late 1800s to the early 1900s. Anton

Wilson is also looking into this for us, but he suggested we speak to you as well."

"Interesting," Felix mused, stroking his chin thoughtfully. "Well, I can certainly point you in the right direction. Please, follow me."

As they walked through the maze of shelves and artifacts, Lin felt a thrill of excitement. She loved the sense of history that clung to every corner of the old building, the stories hidden within its walls just waiting to be discovered. It was the perfect place to begin unraveling the tangled threads of their new mystery.

"Here we are," Felix announced, stopping before a towering shelf filled to the brim with leather-bound books. He ran a slender finger along the spines, finally selecting two that looked particularly old. "These might have what you need. They're a collection of news articles from the early 1900s, but there are more that have been digitized so you can access those on the computers."

"Thanks, Felix. We'll start with these," Lin said gratefully, reaching for one of the heavy volumes. She carefully opened the cover and began to leaf through the yellowed pages.

"Anytime," Felix replied, a warm smile spreading across his face. "I'm always happy to assist fellow seekers of knowledge. Let me know when you need to be set up on the computers. Wave me over if you need any further assistance," the librarian offered kindly, watching the pair as they poured over the old records, "and remember, sometimes the most important clues are hidden in plain sight."

"Thanks," Lin replied, shooting him a smile. "We'll keep that in mind." She scanned the faded text, searching for any mention of fires that might be connected to their current investigation while Viv did the same with the second volume.

"Here we go," Lin said at last, pointing to a passage detailing several suspicious fires that had occurred on the island decades earlier. "This looks promising."

"It sure does," Viv agreed, leaning in to examine the page more closely. "Maybe we'll find a link to today's fires."

"It's too soon to say for sure," Lin admitted. "We'll keep our fingers crossed."

As they delved deeper into the historical records, Lin felt like they were being drawn into a web where the strands connecting the past to the present were growing ever tighter. Her fingers traced the column of faded text, searching for any mention of fires connected to the one at David's house, the one on

Orange Street, or the one in the Cliff neighborhood. The musty smell of the old books and documents filled her nostrils as she scanned the pages. Viv sat beside her cousin, her eyes studying the records.

"Ugh, why isn't this easier?" Viv complained under her breath. "It's like looking for a needle in a haystack."

"I know," Lin murmured, not taking her eyes off the page in front of her, "but we'll find something eventually, I hope."

After an hour had passed, the afternoon light filtering through the windows began to fade over the walls lined with shelves of bound volumes and stacks of papers. With Felix's help logging them into the database, the cousins sat at the bank of computers to continue their search. The silence of the historical society library was broken only by the rustle of paper and the occasional creak of a floorboard. Another hour passed, and Lin's and Viv's eyes began to blur from staring at the tiny print for so long.

"Wait, look at this," Lin said, her voice barely above a whisper. "There was a fire back in 1901. And listen to this: 'Despite a thorough investigation, no suspect has been identified, and the case remains open.' It must have been arson. There isn't any more information though."

Viv waved Felix over and asked him if he could find any more about the fire.

The man sat, pulled the keyboard closer to him, and began to tap away. "I can do some cross-referencing to other articles so we can look for follow-up stories on the fire." A minute later, Felix made a face. "Odd. I'm not finding anything."

"Maybe we should come back another day," Viv said, her voice strained with fatigue. "I'm beat."

"That's probably a good idea," Lin admitted as she rubbed her temples. "I guess we should call it a day."

"I'll do some more searching," Felix told them. "It's possible the news articles we're looking for have been lost to time, but I'll give you a call if I find anything."

The cousins thanked the man and headed out of the library.

"It wasn't a total loss." Lin tried to be upbeat. "We learned there was a house fire in 1901 that was considered arson."

"It's a start." Viv nodded. "It's more than we knew before we got here."

"I'll talk to Anton about it. Maybe he can help us find out who owned that house."

As the sun headed toward the horizon, the cousins walked along the brick sidewalks of town, and Lin glanced around hoping to see the new ghost lurking somewhere nearby, but the shimmering spirit was nowhere to be seen.

We'll find out more tomorrow, she promised herself.

5

As Lin and Viv approached Anton's antique Cape-style house, darkness was taking over and shadows spread on the stone path that led to the front door. The scent of lilacs hung heavy in the air, their deep purple blossoms framing the windows of the charming house.

"Ready to dive into the research?" Viv asked with a warm smile, pulling a notebook and pen from her bag.

Lin felt the familiar thrill of curiosity tingle down her spine. "Absolutely. Let's do this." She raised her hand and knocked on the blue wooden door. Moments later, it creaked open and Anton Wilson greeted them.

"Ah, Lin and Viv," the man's voice was voice

warm and friendly. He stepped aside, gesturing for them into the cozy interior. "Please, come in."

"Thanks," Lin replied, stepping inside.

"The house looks lovely with the May flowers in bloom," Viv remarked, and Anton beamed with pride, clearly pleased with the compliment.

"Thank you. It's taken me years to get the landscaping the way I've wanted it," he explained, leading them down a hallway lined with bookshelves to the library. "I'm not as talented as Lin and Leonard so it takes me ages to get the yardwork done." He glanced at Lin. "Thankfully, I have you to do the weeding, mowing, and trimming."

"You do a great job with the flowers," Lin told him. "The garden looks really pretty."

"Shall we get started?" Anton asked, pushing open a door at the end of the hall. The room beyond was warmly lit with lamps set on a long wooden table next to a desk. A fireplace graced one wall and a brown leather sofa and two armchairs flanked it. "Can I get you something to drink before we begin?"

The cousins declined, eager to get into the research.

"You found something in your newspaper collections?" Lin asked.

Anton's eyes shone with enthusiasm. "Somewhere among these news articles lies the key to our mystery." He gestured for Lin and Viv to join him at the table which was already strewn with several open newspapers and the man's laptop. "I've taken the liberty of pulling some articles that I think might be relevant to the investigation."

As Lin took her seat and looked over the old papers, she knew that within them were stories that had been all but forgotten by the world, and she hoped they might hold the potential to unlock the secret of their new ghost.

"Show us what you found," Lin said.

"Ah, here it is." Anton carefully unfolded a brittle page displaying an article in bold print. "This might shed some light on our ghostly friend."

Lin's eyes narrowed as she leaned closer to read the news article from long ago. "House Fire Claims Lives of Family; Arson Suspected," Lin read the headline.

Viv's hand instinctively reached for her throat; her eyes filled with sadness.

Lin's gaze darted over the lines of text, taking in every detail of the tragic story.

Anton spoke, his voice low and somber. "The fire claimed the lives of William Johnson, his wife Abigail, and their two young children. The blaze was believed to have been set intentionally." He pushed his eyeglasses up to the bridge of his nose. "The arsonist was never found," he continued. "Though there were rumors it was a disgruntled business partner or perhaps a servant with a grudge, no one knows for sure. There are no mentions of any leads or a resolution to the case, but that information may be lost to history. The fire started just after midnight," he said. "William and his family were asleep on the second floor. The arsonist likely broke into the attached barn, spread kerosene on the floor, and lit it."

"But why?" Viv asked. "Revenge? Jealousy? Greed?"

"Maybe that's what William's trying to tell us," Lin suggested. "He wants us to find out who was responsible for his death and the destruction of his home." She could see the ghost in her mind's eye – a tall, gaunt figure with haunted eyes. "William Johnson," she repeated softly.

"Do you think Mr. Johnson is our ghost?" Viv asked.

"It seems likely," Anton replied, nodding gravely. "The timeline matches up, and it would explain why he remains on the island after all these years.

William might be seeking justice for his family's untimely deaths."

"But how will justice be served?" Viv questioned. "The arsonist lived over one hundred years ago."

"It might be enough that the arsonist's name be known," Anton suggested.

Lin stared at the photograph accompanying the article – a charred, blackened shell of what was once a beautiful Colonial-style home. Her heart clenched at the thought of the pain and anguish William must have felt, watching his entire world go up in flames.

"Look at the date," Lin whispered, her finger pointing to the faded ink. "1901. This happened over a century ago, and still, William's spirit lingers."

"The poor man," Viv murmured. "His poor family. I can't believe someone would do such a horrible thing."

Lin reread the article as she committed each detail to memory. "Born in 1864, married with two children. There must be something about him that links him to the arsonist who killed them. Or maybe it was simply random?"

"Let's look at his family," Viv suggested. "Maybe there's a link there we haven't seen yet."

"Good idea." Anton adjusted his eyeglasses, moved

his laptop closer, and tapped at the keyboard, pulling up a vast collection of historical records. "This is the Nantucket census from 1900. We can cross-reference the names mentioned in the article to learn more about William's life and the people he was close to."

As Anton stared at the screen, Lin felt an electric charge in the air that told her they were on the right track.

"Here we are," Anton said, stopping at a page filled with names and occupations. "William Johnson, his wife Abigail, and their children, Henry and Lillian."

"Can we find out anything about where William worked?" Viv asked, leaning over Anton's shoulder to get a better look at the page.

Anton nodded, stood, and headed to the bookshelves. "It would likely be mentioned in one of my books on Nantucket industries. Let me see."

As Anton disappeared into the depths of his library, Lin's thoughts returned to William's ghost and the anguish he must have felt watching his family perish in the flames. She shuddered.

"Anton," Viv called suddenly, her voice tinged with urgency, "I found something. There's a witness account here."

Anton hurried to the table and scanned the

online pages of a local newspaper from 1901. "Read it to us."

"It says, 'Mr. Samuel Thompson, who resides two houses down from the Johnson family, reported seeing a slender figure fleeing the scene shortly after the fire started. He could not provide a clear description but claimed the figure moved with unnatural swiftness.'"

"Unnatural swiftness?" Lin echoed, her brows knitting together in thought. "What in the world does that mean?"

"It means the man was fast." Viv smiled. "What else could it mean? I think I'll be using that phrase from time to time."

As the night wore on, the atmosphere in the room grew heavy.

"Wait," Anton said, holding up a faded letter. "This might be something. It was written by Abigail Johnson to her sister." He read aloud, "'My dear sister, I fear for our family's safety. There have been threats made against us.'"

Lin spoke softly, her pulse quickening. "What could the Johnsons have done to warrant such a threat?"

"Whatever it was," Viv murmured, rubbing her temples as if trying to ward off an impending headache, "things didn't end well for William and his family."

"Keep reading, Anton," Lin urged, her voice laced with anticipation.

The man's eyes returned to the letter. "'I pray we can resolve this matter before tragedy befalls us all. Yours always, Abigail.'"

"Threats against the family?" Lin mused, her mind racing with possibilities. "Maybe someone held a grudge against them? We're definitely onto something here."

As they poured over the materials, Lin had the feeling that they were being watched – not by each other, but by unseen eyes. She shivered, goosebumps prickling along her arms. She glanced around the room looking for the ghost, but he wasn't there.

"I remember finding this information when I was doing research on the island's industries," Anton said, his voice low and urgent. He held up a brittle newspaper clipping detailing a feud between two prominent men – William Johnson and Arthur Radcliffe. "It says here that the dispute began over a business deal gone awry."

Viv's eyes widened with excitement.

Anton said, "There are mentions that the men

were involved in some sort of partnership that went wrong."

Lin leaned closer, her heart pounding as the pieces began to fall into place. "This might be exactly what we've been looking for." She glanced at Viv and Anton, their faces illuminated by the lamplight. "If we can find information about their partnership and the events leading up to the fire, we'll be one step closer to solving this mystery."

Anton agreed. "And hopefully, the ghost will be able to finally lay his soul to rest."

When they returned to reading the old documents, Lin's finger traced the faded ink of an old letter, her eyes narrowing as she tried to make out the looping script. The musty smell of aged paper filled the air around them as Viv shuffled through stacks of documents and Anton studied a delicate photograph with a magnifying glass.

"Look at this," Lin said, holding up a tattered journal. "It has entries made by Arthur Radcliffe himself."

"Really?" Viv replied. "Let's see if there's anything that might give us a clue."

"Anton, you should take a look, too," Lin suggested, handing the journal to the historian. His practiced hands gently flipped through the pages, pausing occasionally to examine passages more closely.

"Wait, listen to this," Anton said after a moment. "'I fear my dealings with Johnson have gone beyond what I initially intended.'"

Lin whispered, sharing a glance with Viv, "He must be talking about William."

"I bet he is," Viv replied, nodding.

"Very well." Anton continued, his voice steady, "'I've decided to confront him tomorrow night, but I worry about the consequences. If only our association had never begun.' The entry ends there."

"Confrontation..." Lin mused, rubbing her forehead. "That could have been the catalyst for the fire."

"It's possible," Anton agreed solemnly, "but we need more evidence to support that theory."

"Right," Viv chimed in.

Lin said, "Let's go back to those newspaper clippings. There may be something we missed."

The trio delved deeper into the piles of information, their minds racing with possibilities. Each piece of evidence seemed to open another door, leading them closer to the truth. Another hour passed as they examined Anton's collection and the online databases.

"Look what I found," Viv exclaimed, holding up a

newspaper article. "It's about a second witness who saw someone leaving the Johnson house just after the fire started."

"Really?" Lin asked, taking the article from Viv and scanning the text.

Anton leaned in to read over Lin's shoulder. "It says the witness described the person as 'wearing a dark coat and hat and having a limp in their step.'" The historian looked up. "Arthur Radcliffe had a limp. I recall reading that in one of his letters."

"Then it's possible that Arthur was at the scene of the fire," Viv whispered, her voice filled with excitement.

"Let's not jump to conclusions yet," Anton cautioned. "We still need more evidence to piece everything together, but we're getting closer."

"Come on, let's keep going," Lin said, her voice filled with resolve. She carefully leafed through another stack of documents.

"Hey, look at this picture," Viv whispered, her eyes wide with discovery as she held up an old photograph. It showed a solemn-looking man dressed in early 20th-century attire, his eyes seemingly staring straight at them. "This could be him. This could be William Johnson."

"Let me see." Anton peered at the photograph,

adjusting his glasses. "Yes, it does resemble the description we have of him. Good find, Viv." He turned to Lin. "Does this man look like your ghost?"

"He does." Lin's mind raced with theories and ideas, and then she felt the hair on the back of her neck stand up. Suddenly, the temperature of the room seemed to drop a few degrees. Goosebumps covered her arms, and she knew without looking that they were no longer alone. She spoke, her voice barely audible. "He's here. William is here with us."

Viv and Anton exchanged worried glances, but remained silent, allowing Lin to focus on the ghostly presence.

"William," Lin called out softly, "we're trying to uncover the truth about your death and the fire. Can you help us in some way?"

The air grew colder still, and Lin sensed the ghost in the room, but he didn't make himself visible. As the chill in the room dissipated, Lin turned to Viv and Anton. "He's gone."

"I have to say I'm not sorry," Viv told them. "I'm always afraid they're going to do something to us."

"Did he communicate anything to you?" Anton asked.

"He didn't." Lin sighed.

Anton tapped his chin. "I remember from my

earlier research that William Johnson owned a successful shipping company back then. He and Arthur Radcliffe might have partnered to expand the business. I'll see if I can find anything about it."

For another hour, the three friends sifted through countless articles, letters, and journals, each one a piece of the puzzle that would hopefully lead them to the identity of the arsonist.

"Look at this," Anton said suddenly, turning his laptop to show an online article with several photographs of a tattered journal embossed with the initials 'W.J.' "I found an entry from William where he mentions a heated argument with Arthur. He doesn't say what it was about, but there's definitely tension between them."

"Arthur could very well be the arsonist," Lin said aloud, her heart racing at the thought. "Did he betray his friend for some reason?"

"Anything's possible," Viv replied, her brow furrowing as she considered the implications. "We need to learn more about Arthur and his relationship with William."

Anton said, "But that might be a very difficult task to achieve." A few minutes later, the man leaned closer to his laptop. "Here's a letter from Arthur Radcliffe to a mutual business associate. He blamed

William Johnson for recommending a poor investment that caused his financial ruin."

"Motive, means, and opportunity," Viv said with a grim smile. "It seems Mr. Radcliffe might have had them all."

The three exchanged glances. Accusing a man of murder was no small thing, even if he had been dead for over a century. They would have to be extremely careful; check and double-check every detail. Only when they had irrefutable proof would they be able to reveal the truth about what happened that fateful night so long ago.

"We still haven't found any follow-up articles reporting on whether the arsonist was found or not," Anton pointed out. "I'll look into that more tomorrow."

Lin stood up and stretched, her joints sore from hours hunched over documents. "We should break for the night. This has been a long day, and we'll need fresh eyes to review any more evidence."

Viv nodded. "You're right. We've made great progress, but there's a lot more to do."

"Thank you, Anton." Lin hugged the man. "We appreciate your help more than we can say." She gave him a tired smile. Her mind buzzed with theories and questions, and she doubted sleep would come easily.

"The pleasure was mine." Anton's eyes crinkled at the corners. "Solving a century-old mystery is quite the exciting event. I look forward to seeing this through to the end with you."

Lin smiled, warmth flooding her chest.

The crisp night air was refreshing after hours cooped up inside. A few stars peeked through the inky black sky and the moon shone its light over the road.

As they walked home, Lin said, "I keep thinking about William Johnson. What he must have gone through, he and his family dying like that in a fire, and now, all these years later, it seems we have a clue. Arthur Radcliffe might have been the arsonist who killed William and his family."

"I know." Viv squeezed Lin's hand. "Sometimes this work we do hits a little too close to home, but I hope we can help bring William some closure. We should take comfort in that."

The words resonated with Lin. She had been given a gift, to see what others couldn't. With that gift came responsibility—to seek the truth, defend the helpless, and find justice for those who could no longer find it for themselves.

It was a duty Lin took seriously, and in that moment, despite the fatigue and emotional turmoil, she felt at peace with the path she walked.

They had uncovered secrets hidden for over a hundred years. They knew who the victims were; now it was time to determine the killer and link it all to the recent island fires.

6

The warm May sun blazed down on Cisco Beach's powdery white sand and turned the ocean into a shimmering turquoise canvas. Lin stood at the water's edge, taking in the lovely scene as the gentle waves lapped at her toes. Beside her, Jeff slathered sunscreen on his arms while Viv and John set up their paddleboards nearby.

"Come on, Lin," Viv called out, grinning broadly as she waded into the water with her paddleboard. "The water's perfect."

Lin couldn't help but smile back at her cousin's enthusiasm. She picked up her own board and followed her cousin, the warmth of the sun on her back and the cool water on her legs. They paddled further out, laughing and chatting.

"All right, team, let's see who can catch the biggest wave," John challenged, flashing a playful grin at the others.

"Bring it on!" Lin replied, determination shining in her eyes.

They spread out across the water, jockeying for position as they waited for the next set of waves. The tension of competition hung in the air, but it was the kind that brought them closer together, not pushed them apart. When the waves finally came, they dug their paddles into the water with gusto, propelling themselves forward with powerful strokes.

As Lin rode the crest of her wave, she could hear Viv's triumphant whoop and Jeff's good-natured groan as he wiped out behind her.

"Whoa, nice one, Lin!" Viv called out as they both paddled back toward John, who was already waiting for them.

"Thanks! That was so much fun!" Lin replied, her face flushed from the exhilaration of the ride.

"Definitely," Jeff agreed, finally catching up to them, water dripping from his soaked hair. "Let's do it again."

They rode the waves, over and over, losing themselves in the fun of playing in the warm ocean waves. The sun continued its steady climb, casting ever-changing patterns of light and shadow on the water around them. For a time, there were no ghosts and no mysteries, just four family members enjoying the sun and sea.

"Okay, last one," John announced after they had ridden several more waves.

"I'm ready," Lin said, feeling the ache of tired muscles setting in. "Let's make this one count."

They exchanged determined nods before setting off once more, paddles slicing through the water as they raced to catch the perfect wave. With the sun on her face and salt on her lips, Lin could feel the familiar thrill building inside her as she matched her companions stroke-for-stroke.

After riding the waves, John and Jeff paddled toward shore while Lin and Viv stayed out a little longer. The sun beat down on Lin's shoulders as she paddled through the waters of the southern end of the island. Above them, seagulls wheeled and cried while the gentle waves lapped at her paddleboard.

After days of researching old newspapers and historical records, it felt glorious to be outside. Lin breathed in the fresh, salty air.

Viv came up beside her, water streaming from her hair. "Isn't this perfect? I really needed this."

Lin dipped her paddle in the water, adjusting her

course. "Me, too. It's too easy to get bogged down by work, errands, and everything else, and I was starting to see arsonists and ghosts in every shadow."

"Well, don't look now, but I think there's a ghost shark following you," Viv teased.

Lin whipped around, heart leaping, before she caught Viv's impish grin. "Very funny."

"Gotcha." Viv cackled.

Lin shook her head and closed her eyes for a moment, soaking in the sun and enjoying the moment. The gentle rocking of the waves lulled her into a peaceful mood.

Suddenly, a splash of cold water shocked her from her reverie. She sputtered, opening her eyes to find Viv grinning at her, pleased with herself for having splashed a big handful of ocean water at her cousin.

"Gotcha again." Viv laughed.

Lin couldn't keep from smiling. "You're really terrible."

"But you love me anyway," Viv said with a cheeky grin.

"Lucky for you," Lin shot back. She splashed a wave of water at Viv, who shrieked and paddled away, laughter trailing behind her.

Lin shook her head and paddled back to shore,

and the two of them headed for their sand chairs and towels. Viv, ever the protective one, handed out water bottles to everyone, ensuring they stayed hydrated in the unusual May heat.

"Thanks, hon," John said as he wrapped an arm around Viv's waist. His short hair was damp from the ocean, and his eyes sparkled with a mix of affection and mischief. "So," John said as he dried off, "I've got good news. I found a rental for David and Noelle. They can stay until the end of the summer or for the rest of the year."

Lin glanced at John with a smile. The Winchesters had lost their home in the arson fire that had nearly claimed David's life. "I'm so glad to hear you've found them a new place."

John said, "David was discharged from the hospital yesterday, and Noelle wants to get him settled somewhere familiar so they're staying on-island."

"David really does need more time to recuperate from the smoke inhalation," Viv agreed, her voice tinged with concern. "He's only just been discharged from the hospital, and I know Noelle is beyond grateful that you found them somewhere to stay for the rest of the year."

"Ah, well, it's the least I could do." John shrugged

modestly, rubbing the back of his neck. "I'm glad something suitable came on the market."

Jeff grunted. "At least whoever's behind these fires won't know where they're staying now." Thinking of the fire, his mouth twisted into a frown. "Small comfort, I know, but every little bit helps."

"That's a good point," Viv said. She shot Lin a worried look. They hadn't yet told their husbands about the details regarding the connection between the recent fires and the historical arson case from over a century ago. "Hopefully whoever is responsible for the fires this month will be caught soon."

"The rental should at least give David and Noelle a temporary refuge," John said. "It's a big house, two stories with a balcony overlooking the water. Noelle said the view alone will do wonders for David's recovery."

"That sounds perfect," Lin said. "Please tell them we're glad they'll have a comfortable place to stay and to let us know if there's anything we can do for them."

"I will," John promised.

Viv said, "We think we may have a lead on the identity of the ghost. William Johnson, a wealthy businessman, died in a fire at his home in 1901 along with his wife and two children. We believe his business partner, Arthur Radcliffe, may have been responsible for the fire."

"We found an old newspaper article describing the fire and Mr. Radcliffe's financial troubles," Lin added. "It seems he lost most of his fortune not long before the fire. We want to look into the Radcliffe family history and see if there are any descendants still on the island who might know some of the family lore."

"That's a good lead," Jeff said with a nod. "What can we do to help?"

Lin said, "Jeff, do you think, with your restoration company contacts, you could find any information on the recent house fires? Maybe there's a pattern we're missing."

"Absolutely," Jeff told her, his eyes meeting hers. "I'll ask around. I'll see what I can find out."

With a serious expression, John said, "We have to be careful. Whoever is responsible for these recent fires might not want their secrets uncovered. We don't want our homes to become targets."

"I had the same thought," Viv told her husband. "We'll be very careful."

Lin smiled. "We'll let you know if we need any more help. For now, we're just doing research."

While Jeff and John grabbed a Frisbee and

headed for an empty area of the beach, Lin took a deep breath and let it out slowly. She dug her feet under the sand, and it felt soft between her toes. It was the perfect beach day, but her mind was still churning with the details of the case.

She glanced over at Viv, who was gazing pensively out at the waves. No doubt her thoughts were focused on the mystery as well.

"I can't stop thinking about it," Viv said quietly, voicing Lin's own thoughts. "About the ghost, and the fires, and whether we're really on the right track with the Radcliffe angle." She hugged her knees to her chest, frown lines creasing her forehead.

"I feel the same way," Lin admitted, "but we have a good lead. We just have to follow it."

"You're right." Viv sighed. "I just wish we had more to go on. Talking to the Radcliffe descendants seems like a shot in the dark."

"We have to start somewhere," Lin said. "This is the best theory we have so far."

"I know." Viv glanced over at Jeff and John, who were tossing the Frisbee back and forth, bare chests gleaming with sunscreen and sweat. "At least we have Libby and Anton, and our husbands to help. I don't know what I'd do if we had to handle this on our own."

"Me neither." Lin smiled, pride welling in her chest at the thought of her caring husband and friends.

"We should start planning our next moves," Viv said, "interviewing the Radcliffes and looking into the recent fires. The sooner we dig in, the sooner we can solve this case and put that ghost to rest."

Lin sighed, sinking into the comfort of her beach chair.

Beside her, Viv closed her eyes behind her sunglasses. "We needed this, a chance to recharge before diving back in."

Lin hummed, grabbing a sandwich from the cooler, turkey and cheddar on hearty bread. Her stomach rumbled in anticipation.

"Did you remember the pickles this time?" Viv asked, cracking an eye open.

Lin grinned. "Of course. What kind of cousin do you think I am?"

"The best kind." Viv sat up, stretching her arms over her head.

Lin passed her cousin a sandwich, enjoying the companionable silence as they ate.

After a few moments, Jeff and John wandered over to join them, flopping into the empty chairs. Jeff's hand found Lin's, their fingers lacing together.

She smiled at him, warmth spreading through her veins.

"How was the game?" Lin asked.

"I beat him soundly," John announced.

"In your dreams." Jeff snorted, though his eyes twinkled with mirth. "I was going easy on him."

"Uh huh." Lin looked at John, who was studiously avoiding her gaze. "How about it? Did Jeff go easy on you?"

"Of course not," John scoffed, though his cheeks flushed pink. "I won fair and square."

Laughter bubbled up in Lin's chest at the obvious lie. She shook her head.

"We're too clever for your tricks, John." Viv grinned at her husband, patting his knee. "But it's all right. We still love you, even if you can't beat Jeff at Frisbee without cheating."

"Ganging up on me now, are you?" But John was smiling, wrapping an arm around Viv's shoulders and pressing a kiss to her temple.

Waves lapped the shore, a warm breeze blew gently, and birds skittered across the damp sand, retreating from the incoming tide.

Lin closed her eyes, listening to the idle chatter of her companions, the cries of seabirds, and the rhythm of the waves. The mystery they faced seemed far away, but Lin knew it was only a reprieve, not an end to the dilemma. The ghost was still out there, needing her help. With a sigh, she opened her eyes. "We should head back," she said softly. "It's getting late."

Nods and sounds of agreement met her words. As a group, they began packing up chairs, towels, umbrellas, and the remains of their picnic. John helped Viv haul their paddleboards onto the roof of his truck while Lin and Jeff shook out towels and folded chairs.

As the sun dipped lower, together, they made their way off the beach and back to town, refreshed and ready to continue the investigation.

7

It was a warm sunny day as Lin and Viv approached the neatly-tended Cape Cod style house, their arms laden with bags of groceries and a couple of dinners. The scent of freshly mown grass and the distant sound of people chatting together on the sidewalk drifted through the air, hiding the fact that this was a home that had seen more than its fair share of tragedy in recent months.

"Such a terrible shame, isn't it?" Viv whispered to Lin, her eyes welling up. "First Meredith, and then Peter so soon after."

Lin nodded; her heart heavy with the weight of the Hunter family's misfortunes. Just three months ago, the mother, Meredith, had lost her battle with cancer. Then, as if fate hadn't been cruel enough,

Peter Hunter met an untimely end in a car accident only a month after his wife died, leaving their three children orphaned and struggling to cope.

As they reached the front door, Paul, the eldest of the siblings at twenty-two, welcomed them in with a weary smile. His brown eyes seemed older than his years, framed by dark circles that told of sleepless nights spent worrying for his family's future. The strong, protective nature he'd inherited from his father had kicked into high gear since the loss of both parents.

"Thanks for coming, Viv, Lin," he said, stepping aside to allow them in.

"Of course, Paul. We're happy to help out," Viv responded warmly, her voice laced with genuine concern.

Inside, the house was immaculate, yet every corner seemed to hold a hint of melancholy. Beth, aged twenty-one, came out of the kitchen, wiping her hands on a dish towel. She'd always been a nurturing person and was now trying to keep some bit of normalcy for her younger brother amid the new chaos of their lives.

"Hey, Viv, Lin. How are you?" Beth asked.

"Doing well, thanks," Lin replied, giving her a reassuring smile. "How about you?"

Beth shrugged. She'd been torn between finishing her final upcoming year of college and finding work to help support the family since their parents' deaths. The stress of the decision was etched across her delicate features, which once showed a lively, carefree spirit that seemed to have vanished.

"Taking it one day at a time," she answered softly.

"Brian's in the backyard," Paul interjected, his voice tired but determined. "He's been working part-time on weekends and some days after school with the harbor master, trying to bring in some extra money. Once school is out, he wants to up his hours, but I don't think that's a good idea. He's fourteen. He shouldn't be working all the time."

"He's a good kid. He wants to help out, but like you said, he should spend time with his friends and not work all summer," Lin said.

Beth, Lin, and Viv carried the groceries to the kitchen.

Lin said, "We brought a couple of dinners, beef stew and chicken tacos. It should hold you for a couple of days."

Beth put some things in the fridge and the rest into the cupboards. "We really appreciate it. This whole situation is exhausting."

As they returned to the living room, they settled on the sofas and the conversation turned to the financial struggles the siblings were facing. Their father's gambling addiction had left the family with a mountain of debt, and the stress of dealing with bill collectors and late notices was taking its toll on the young adults.

"Is there anything we can do to help?" Viv asked after hearing the details of their situation. "Anything at all?"

"Your kindness means more than you know," Paul replied, his voice cracking from the strain. "The meals and groceries you and the other neighbors bring us are a godsend, and it really helps to know we're not alone."

"We all want to do what we can to help out," Viv reassured them, squeezing Beth's hand for emphasis. "We know you'd do it for any of us."

"Thank you," Beth whispered, a few tears spilling down her cheeks. "It means so much."

Lin turned to Beth and then to Paul, her voice gentle. "I can't imagine the weight on your shoulders right now, but I just want you to know how much we all admire what you're both doing for your family."

Paul's gaze drifted toward the window, his eyes settling on the neatly-tended garden beyond. He had taken on the role of head of household in the wake of their parents' passing, working to become his fourteen-year-old brother's legal guardian and fighting to maintain a sense of normalcy for his siblings. Becoming Brian's legal guardian and keeping the family home had become his primary focus.

"Thanks, Lin," he replied with a half-hearted smile, his voice heavy. "Just trying to do what our parents would have wanted, you know?"

"Let us know if we can do more than bring groceries and meals," Viv chimed in, her warm eyes filled with admiration.

"Thank you," Paul said softly, nodding in gratitude as he turned back to face them.

The Hunter siblings' trauma was etched into every aspect of their lives since the tragic loss of their parents. Sleepless nights spent tossing and turning, haunted by vivid nightmares, left Paul and Beth feeling exhausted. Their once-happy laughter had been replaced by a hollow silence, punctuated only by the occasional sniffle or shaky breath.

"Have the three of you considered seeking counseling to help process your grief?" Lin asked cautiously, searching their faces for any hint of resistance.

Beth toyed with the frayed edge of the throw pillow in her lap, her fingers trembling slightly. "We've thought about it, but ... well, with everything going on, it's just hard to find the time."

"Or the money," Paul added, his jaw clenching as he thought of the mounting debts that threatened to bury them. "I'm not sure if our insurance will cover it, and I haven't had time to look into it."

"That's understandable," Lin acknowledged, her gaze sympathetic, "but it's important to prioritize your mental health. How about I look into it for you? I can see what resources are available."

"I think that's a good idea," Beth whispered as she glanced toward Paul.

"Okay," Paul agreed after a moment. "That would be really helpful."

"Good," Viv said, nodding in approval. "Would it help if I set you up with my financial planner? She could go over your debts and income and help you figure out what to do. You might not be responsible for your parents' debts at all."

"That would be amazing," Paul said as his young brother Brian came in to join them in the living room.

As they sat together, they chatted about island happenings, Brian's last few weeks of school before summer vacation, and Paul's graduation from college.

"You're planning to go to your graduation ceremony, aren't you?" Lin asked.

Paul shrugged. "I don't think so. There's too much going on."

"You really should go. Mark the occasion. Take a break. Celebrate your accomplishment." Lin gave him a nod.

"I'll see."

Viv beamed at the young man. "I heard you got a job with a local engineering firm. That's great news."

Paul forced a smile, hoping his fatigue didn't show too clearly. "Yeah, I was lucky to find something so close to home. With my degree in civil engineering, I can help design and build infrastructure right here on Nantucket. It should provide some financial stability for us."

"Congratulations, Paul," Viv added, her warm smile reaching her eyes. "That's really impressive."

"Thanks," he replied, rubbing the back of his neck. Despite the praise, he couldn't help feeling overwhelmed. The weight of responsibility on his shoulders seemed to grow heavier each day.

Beth glanced at her older brother, her expression softening with concern. "You're doing so much for us already. You have to remember to take care of yourself, too."

"Speaking of which..." Viv hesitated before continuing. "I'm sorry to bring it up, but we heard about your breakup with Jessica. Are you holding up okay?"

Paul's heart clenched at the mention of his ex-girlfriend. He hadn't seen it coming. One minute they'd been making plans for their future together, and the next she'd ended things, claiming she couldn't handle the stress of his situation.

"Yeah, it's fine," he said, shrugging nonchalantly, though the ache in his chest pained him. "Just one more thing to deal with, I guess." He looked down, his hands in his lap. Just once, he wished he could let his guard down, to admit how much everything hurt, but now as the head of the family, he couldn't afford that luxury. "Really, it's fine," he repeated, forcing another smile. "I've got enough on my plate without worrying about a relationship right now."

As the conversation shifted to lighter topics, Paul's thoughts stayed on Jessica and the void she'd left behind. The pressure seemed relentless sometimes — managing the household, caring for his siblings, and dealing with the emotional fallout of losing both their parents. And now, facing heartbreak on top of it all.

Beth was quiet and her shoulders were hunched, her hands wringing in her lap as she thought about her future. The weight of the decision that lay ahead seemed to press down on her like an invisible burden.

"Have you made up your mind?" Viv asked gently, placing a comforting hand on the younger girl's shoulder.

"No." Beth sighed, her green eyes clouded with uncertainty. "I know I have to do something to help support the family, but I can't decide whether it's better to finish my last year of college or find a job right away. If I finish my degree, I'll have more job opportunities and potentially a higher salary, but we need money now, and there's no guarantee I'll find a good job after graduation. And then there's the cost of the tuition."

"Those are tough choices," Viv agreed, "but remember you have options. You don't necessarily have to choose between school and work – maybe you could find a part-time job while you finish your degree?"

"Maybe," Beth conceded, though she didn't

sound entirely convinced. She glanced at Paul. "What do you think I should do?"

Paul paused for a moment as his eyes met hers, filled with concern and understanding. "Ultimately, it's your decision," he said softly, "but whatever you choose, I'll support you. It might be best if you finish your degree. Your earnings will be higher if you have your bachelor's degree, and that will impact your life for the better."

Beth's gaze dropped to the coffee table. "It's been tough though. We're barely making ends meet with the little bit of savings we have, and with Paul's job just starting, we haven't had much of a cushion to fall back on."

"Brian's been feeling it, too," Paul interjected, his voice strained. "He's had to give up some of his extracurricular activities so he can do a few hours of work a week at the harbor."

"That's really rough," Lin murmured sympathetically.

"Sometimes it feels like we're drowning in it all," Beth confessed, her voice barely above a whisper, "but we have to keep going. For each other. Things will get better."

Viv agreed, squeezing Beth's hand reassuringly. "You'll find a way through this. I know you will."

"Actually," Brian spoke up, "there's a support group at school. I've been going to their meetings. It's ... nice to talk to other kids who've lost someone or who are having issues."

"Good for you, Brian," Lin encouraged, proud of the young boy for seeking out help. "It's so important to have people around who understand what you're going through."

Viv chimed in, eager to remind the siblings that they weren't alone. "You know the whole neighborhood has rallied around you, right? We're all here to support you."

"We know you've organized the meal delivery schedule," Beth said, "with the neighbors taking turns bringing over dinners a few times a week. It's one less thing for us to worry about, and it saves us a lot of money."

"Mrs. Thompson's lasagna is the best," Brian exclaimed, momentarily perking up as he grinned at his siblings. "It tastes just like Mom's because Mom gave Mrs. Thompson her recipe."

Everyone smiled.

Paul was visibly moved by the outpouring of support from their neighbors. "It means more than you know. Sometimes—" He looked around at his siblings. "—it feels like we're navigating this grief with lead weights strapped to our ankles, but knowing that there are people out there who care..." He swallowed hard, his eyes shining. "....it helps. It really does."

"Of course," Viv assured him, reaching over to give his hand a comforting squeeze. "We'll all do what we can for you."

Beth said hesitantly, "We're trying to keep everything together. We can't drift apart. We're all that's left of our family."

"It's so hard sometimes, but we won't let anything pull us apart," Paul told her.

Beth nodded at her brothers. "And that's a promise."

8

Lin stood in Viv's neighborhood at the location of the third fire, scanning the charred remains of the home. The smell of burnt wood filled her nostrils, and she felt a familiar chill run down her spine as she caught sight of the new ghost, his form wavering like smoke against the backdrop of the ruined house.

"Hello. You're William Johnson, aren't you?" Lin said softly. As Lin gazed into the ghost's otherworldly eyes, she felt a connection to him, their shared desire to uncover the truth forming an unspoken bond between them.

A sudden wave of anxiety washed over her, leaving her with the unnerving sensation that the arsonist wasn't done yet. More fires would be set, putting more lives in danger.

"Are you trying to tell me something?" Lin asked, her voice trembling with apprehension. "Do you know who's responsible for these fires?"

William's ghostly form flickered briefly, but he remained silent, his eyes never leaving hers.

"If you know anything, I need your help to stop this before anyone else gets hurt," Lin implored.

The ghost hesitated, then gave the tiniest of nods, acknowledging her request. He began to fade away, his shimmering atoms swirling as he disappeared.

"Lin." Viv's voice broke through her thoughts, pulling her cousin back to reality. "Are you ready to talk to some neighbors?"

"Yes. Let's find out what they know."

As they walked away from the scene of the fire, Lin felt the lingering presence of William Johnson's ghost. "Let's start by talking to the people living closest to the fires," she suggested as they strolled down the quiet street. "They might have seen or heard something."

"I was thinking the same thing," Viv agreed, looking around the neighborhood for potential witnesses who might be outside.

Approaching the first house, Lin noticed an elderly woman sitting on her porch, knitting in the fading afternoon light. She seemed like the perfect person to talk with first – someone who spent a lot of time observing the comings and goings of the neighborhood.

"Excuse me, Mrs. Dolan," Viv called out gently, not wanting to startle the woman. "We're looking into the recent fires in the area. Would it be okay if we ask you some questions?"

"Of course, dear," the old woman replied, putting her knitting aside and adjusting her glasses. "How are you doing, Viv? An arsonist in our neighborhood, can you believe it? It's just awful. I'll help however I can."

"Did you see anything unusual around the time of the fires?" Lin asked.

"Let me think," the woman said, her brow furrowing with concentration. "I did see someone. I told the police what I saw. It was a slender figure in dark clothing. They were skulking around the side of the house before it caught fire, right before the flames appeared. I was up late that night. I couldn't sleep."

"He was wearing dark clothing, you say?" Viv chimed in. "Did you see any distinguishing features? Anything that would help us identify the person?"

The elderly woman shook her head. "I'm afraid

not, dear. My eyesight isn't what it used to be, and it was a dark night. I'm not even sure if it was a man or a woman, but I can tell you they seemed agile, like they knew how to move without drawing attention. They were quick, but quiet."

"Can you remember anything else about them?" Lin questioned.

"Honestly, no. That's all I could see. I recall wondering why they seemed to be so intent on the Winchesters' house. Now we know why."

"Thank you, Mrs. Dolan," Viv said, her mind racing with possibilities. "You've been very helpful."

As Lin and Viv continued down the street, they found another neighbor watering his lawn. He appeared to be in his forties, with a scruffy beard and a baseball cap pulled low over his eyes.

"Hi, Robert," Viv began. "We're looking into the recent fires. Did you see anything unusual or suspicious that night?"

The man scratched his chin thoughtfully. "Well, I did see someone running away from the fire. The person was slim, wore dark clothes, and had a backpack."

"Did you catch a glimpse of their face?" Viv asked eagerly.

"Can't say I did," the man replied, apologetically,

"but they were definitely in a hurry, like they didn't want to stick around."

"Thank you," Lin said, her worry deepening. The descriptions matched, but they still lacked concrete details to identify the arsonist. As they continued their interviews, her mind churned with the information they'd gathered. She knew they needed to find this person before another fire was set, but how?

With the sun beginning to set, Lin and Viv stood once again at the location of the fire. The air was heavy with the scent of charred wood and ash, and the skeletal remains of the once beautiful house loomed like a dark monument.

"William Johnson," Lin whispered, "I need your help."

As if summoned by her words, the ghost of William Johnson appeared before her. Unlike his previous appearances, he now seemed more solid, his features more distinguishable. He wore a neatly pressed suit, his hair slicked back, and a pocket watch dangled from his waistcoat. His eyes held a mixture of sadness and determination as they locked onto Lin's. "He's here," she told her cousin.

"Maybe he'll communicate with you," Viv hoped aloud.

Lin studied the ghost's movements. She noticed

how he seemed to glide effortlessly over the ground, his feet never quite touching the earth beneath him. His hands were almost transparent, yet they occasionally flickered with an otherworldly light.

"Can you tell me anything about who might be setting these fires?" Lin asked, her voice trembling slightly. She knew communication with the ghost was important, but she couldn't help feeling unnerved by his intense stare.

The ghost shook his head slowly, his expression somber. Then, raising a hand, he pointed towards the remnants of the house. Lin followed his gesture and saw, among the rubble, a small, scorched object.

"Is that ... a clue?" she ventured, her heart pounding hard.

"Where? What's he telling you?" Viv questioned.

"I think there's something in the ashes." Lin carefully approached the object, crouching down to get a closer look. It was a half-burned matchbook, the logo of a nearby pub, Smitty's Place, barely visible.

"Did you see who dropped this?" Lin asked, turning back to the ghost.

William Johnson's gaze flickered toward a group of houses further down the street. Lin could tell that he was unable to reveal much information, but she knew that his desire to stop the arsonist and protect others from suffering his fate was foremost in his mind.

Lin murmured, clasping the matchbook in her hand. "We'll figure it out. We'll find the person responsible."

The ghost nodded, his face softening for a moment before he disappeared, leaving Lin standing near the burned-down house.

"Viv," she said, stepping closer to her cousin with her hand outstretched. "I think we might have our first real lead."

"What is it?" Viv's eyes widened.

"Look at this." Lin carefully held up the charred matchbook as if it were a fragile relic. "William is trying to help us. Remember how I mentioned his different expressions and gestures? Well, when he pointed at this matchbook, I could see a sort of urgency in his eyes," Lin explained, her voice hushed. "He knows something we don't, something important."

"Like who set the fires?" Viv ventured.

"Exactly." Lin nodded.

"All right then, let's follow this lead and see where it takes us."

Their next stop was the pub whose logo adorned the matchbook. They entered the dimly lit Smitty's

Place, where the scent of beer lingered in the air. They approached the bartender, a grizzled man with a bushy beard and a tattoo sleeve on one arm.

"Excuse me," Lin began, holding out the matchbook. "We're trying to find out some information about the recent arson fires. Have you seen anyone suspicious hanging around here lately?"

The bartender eyed the burnt object warily before shrugging. "Can't say that I have, but then again, lots of folks pass through here. What's your interest in a burned-up matchbook?"

"A house in my neighborhood was set on fire recently," Viv explained, her voice firm. "We found the matchbook with this pub's logo in the ashes. Someone who was here might be involved."

"Arson." The bartender frowned, stroking his beard thoughtfully. "Well, there was a guy in here a few nights ago. He comes in fairly often. That night he was acting a bit odd. Kept to himself mostly, but I noticed him fiddling with a matchbook at the bar. He seemed antsy, maybe a little anxious."

"Can you describe him?" Lin asked, her pulse quickening.

"A medium build, maybe in his twenties. Dark hair and wore a hoodie. Didn't catch his name. Like I said, I've seen him here before. He's quiet, never causes any trouble."

The bartender's description was similar to the one they'd heard from the neighbors who'd seen someone running away from the fires, except for the man being slender.

"Thank you," Viv said, exchanging a glance with Lin. "We appreciate your help."

As they left the pub, Lin felt a chill run down her spine. She glanced over her shoulder and saw William Johnson standing by the door, his ethereal form flickering like a candle flame in the wind, and his eyes met hers. Although it was clear to her now that he knew more than he could share, she understood the ghost couldn't directly reveal what he knew.

"Viv," Lin whispered. "William is here. I think we're on the right track."

"Maybe he can tell you something else," Viv told her cousin.

"William," Lin addressed the ghost, her voice firm but gentle. "I know you want to prevent others from suffering your fate. Can you give us any more clues about the arsonist?"

The ghost's translucent eyes turned to Lin, and

for a moment, she saw something shift in his expression—an urgency that seemed to say, *I'm trying*.

"Maybe he can't give us the answer outright, but he can guide us," Viv suggested, her tone laced with empathy for the ghost's struggle.

"Can you show us where to look next?" Lin asked, her heart pounding in anticipation.

As if responding to her request, William's gaze shifted to a spot further down the street, but then his form began to dim, and in a moment, he was gone.

"He disappeared. I think he was losing energy. It seems hard for him to stay visible."

Viv's voice vibrated with excitement. "It's okay. We have a piece of evidence now. When William feels stronger, he'll lead you to something else."

Lin smiled at her cousin. "Ever the optimist."

The combined efforts of two determined women and one dedicated ghost would surely be enough to end the worry and fear plaguing their town. And with that, they headed home.

9

The high school auditorium buzzed with excitement as students from freshmen to seniors mingled among the tables set up for the annual career fair. The air was thick with anticipation, and the chatter of youthful voices bounced off the walls, creating a noise that was both fun and overwhelming.

Lin surveyed the scene from her position behind one of the tables, taking in the various displays and the eager faces of the students who drifted from booth to booth. Beside her was her business partner Leonard, and together, they represented their landscaping business, which had earned a reputation as one of the best on Nantucket Island.

"Looks like quite the crowd this year. I can't believe how much it's grown over just the past few years," Lin said amid the background noise. "Maybe we can inspire some of these kids to consider a career in landscaping."

"Maybe that isn't such a great idea. If any of them go into landscaping, they might put us out of business," Leonard kidded, his weathered face creased into a warm smile. He adjusted a stack of brochures that showcased their work, beautiful photographs of lush gardens and carefully maintained lawns serving as examples of their expertise.

As the crowd of students continued to meander through the auditorium, Lin found herself drawn into their energy and enthusiasm. She remembered attending a similar event a very long time ago when she was a teen and before she had discovered her love for landscaping.

A group of students approached their table, their eyes wide and curious as they picked up the brochures and looked over the photographs. Lin answered their questions and offered words of encouragement. She felt a bit of pride as she spoke about her profession, knowing that she had found her calling and built a life for herself that she truly loved.

Beyond the landscaping table, the high school auditorium buzzed with activity as students interacted with professionals from various fields. At one end of the hall, a group of doctors, nurses, and researchers engaged in animated conversations with curious teenagers, explaining the details of their occupations.

Nearby, business people talked about how they got started, the challenges they'd faced, and how they persevered. Engineers displayed blueprints and scale models, discussing the problem-solving and math skills that underpinned their work, while police officers and fishermen shared tales of adventure and danger that seemed to captivate the students.

Amidst the hive of excitement, Lin noticed a familiar face approaching her and Leonard's table. Brian Hunter, the young teen with brown hair and a lanky frame, had always shown an interest in landscaping during his visits to Lin's backyard with his family. His eyes sparkled with curiosity as he approached, and a tentative smile tugged at the corners of his mouth.

"Hey, Lin," Brian greeted, shifting his weight from one foot to the other. "Hi, Leonard." His nervous energy showed his eagerness to learn more about their business.

"Hi there, Brian," Lin replied warmly, sharing a

knowing glance with Leonard. "It's great to see you here. Are you considering a career in landscaping?"

Brian rubbed the back of his neck, his cheeks flushing slightly. "Well, I'm not sure. I've always liked working outdoors, and your gardens always look so great. So, yeah, I thought it'd be cool to learn more about it."

"Landscaping isn't only about making things look pretty," Leonard chimed in, his voice gentle yet firm. "It's also about understanding the science behind it all – the soil, the plants, the climate."

Lin could see the gears turning in Brian's mind as he absorbed this information. She knew that the loss of his parents had taken a mighty toll on him, and she hoped that finding an interest in something like landscaping might help him find some stability.

"Take a brochure," Lin suggested kindly, handing one to Brian. "If you have any questions or want to try your hand at it sometime, just let us know."

"Thanks," Brian said, his voice cracking slightly as he accepted the brochure. His gaze lingered on the photographs before he looked up, gratitude shining in his eyes. "I really appreciate it."

"How's it going working with the harbormaster?" Lin asked.

Brian's eyes lit up. "It's great. She's really nice. It's

fun seeing all the things she has to do in a day." The teen scanned the brochure. "How do you decide which plants work best for different types of soil? And what about harsh weather?"

"Ah, those are excellent questions," Lin replied with a smile. "It's important to consider the native plants of the area when designing a landscape. They've adapted to the local conditions and are more likely to thrive."

"Exactly," Leonard added, rubbing his calloused hands together. "We also study microclimates within a garden. Different areas can have varying levels of sunlight, moisture, and wind, affecting which plants will grow best there."

Brian furrowed his brow, clearly intrigued. As they spoke, Lin observed the teenager's posture relax slightly, his hands no longer fidgeting nervously.

Just then, Sara Harper appeared beside them, her dark curls bouncing as she approached. "Lin! How lovely to see you here," she exclaimed, her eyes sparkling with warmth. Sara was one of Brian's teachers and a close friend of Lin's, their bond forged during long walks along the beach discussing literature and life.

"Hi, Sara," Lin greeted her, noting the teacher's comfortable yet professional attire. The young woman wore black slacks paired with a cream blouse and a colorful scarf draped around her neck. "It's always great to come to career day."

"Absolutely," Sara agreed before turning to Brian. "I'm glad to see you taking an interest in landscaping. It could be a wonderful outlet for your creativity and energy."

"Thanks, Ms. Harper," Brian mumbled as he looked down. "I guess I'll look around some more."

As Brian turned to leave, Lin felt a pang of concern for the young man. She hoped that his interest in a hobby or profession could be the spark he needed to help him overcome the challenges he was facing.

Lin watched as Sara's eyes followed Brian before turning to her. She could tell that her friend was deeply worried about the young man and his struggles in school, but for now, they focused on discussing landscaping tips and island news.

After a few minutes of chatting, Sara's expression turned somber, and she glanced around to ensure that no one else was eavesdropping on their conversation. "Lin, I need to talk to you about Brian," she began in a hushed tone. "I know you're not a relative, but I know you were friendly with his parents. His performance in school is declining rapidly. His grades have dropped, he's neglecting his homework, and he's even been lashing out at his classmates during group projects."

"Really?" Lin replied, her brow furrowing. "Can you give me an example?"

"Last week," Sara confided, "we were working on a group project in Language Arts class, analyzing characters from a novel we'd just finished reading. Brian became unusually agitated when one of his group members disagreed with his interpretation. He slammed his fist on the table and stormed out of the classroom."

"Wow, that doesn't sound like the Brian I know," Lin admitted.

"Exactly," Sara confirmed. "And that's not the only thing. Our school counselor, Mrs. Peterson, has been holding group sessions three times a week for students dealing with grief, loss, or other issues. Brian used to attend regularly, but lately, he's been skipping them."

"Maybe he feels like they're not helping?" Lin suggested, rubbing her forehead as she tried to process the information.

"Maybe," Sara conceded, "but I think there's more to it than that. The sessions are focused on helping students express their emotions and develop coping strategies, such as journaling and mindfulness techniques. It's possible that facing his feelings is becoming too overwhelming for him."

"Or maybe he's feeling isolated," Leonard interjected. "Sometimes, when people are grieving, they pull away from others, even those who can help them." Leonard had done just that after the death of his wife years ago.

"Whatever the reason, I'm growing more and more worried about him," Sara admitted, wringing her hands together. "He's such a bright young man with so much potential. I hate to see him struggling like this."

"Is there anything we can do to help?" Lin asked.

"I don't know," Sara said, hesitating for a moment before continuing. "I think it'll take more than just school resources to get through to Brian. I think he'd benefit from some one-on-one counseling. He needs someone who can lend an ear when he needs it most. It's not always easy to talk to a friend or a relative in a case like this. He might need a counselor who has experience working with people in the throes of grief."

Sara glanced around the bustling auditorium before leaning in closer to Lin and Leonard. "The school contacted Brian's older brother, Paul, to discuss Brian's situation," she shared in a hushed tone. "Paul is doing his best, but he's been struggling as well since their parents passed away. They were all really close."

Lin's heart went out to the siblings who had lost so much. "It must be hard for all of them."

Sara agreed, her eyes filled with concern. "But despite everything, Paul has managed to start a new job and take care of Brian. He's a good guy, just ... overwhelmed."

"Understandable." Leonard nodded sympathetically. "So, what did Paul say when the school reached out to him?"

Sara sighed. "He was appreciative of the support but also frustrated because he doesn't know how to help Brian. He's tried talking to him, encouraging him to attend the group sessions, even offering to go with him, but nothing seems to work."

"Maybe we can come up with some ideas together," Lin suggested, her mind already working on possible solutions. "First off, I think it's important that Brian knows there are a lot of people who care about him and are here for him, not just as authority figures or professionals, but as people who genuinely care about his well-being."

"Good point," Leonard chimed in. "Maybe he

could find activities he enjoys outside of school where he can build connections and gain confidence. It might help with his anger issues, too."

"Great ideas," Sara responded enthusiastically. "Brian mentioned he likes working with the harbormaster so that's a good experience for him. Since he showed interest in landscaping, maybe he could spend some time working with you two? It would give him something productive to do and take his mind off his troubles at the same time."

"Sure," Lin readily agreed. "We'd be more than happy to have him join us on some projects. In fact, we could even teach him a few things, if he's interested."

"That would be great," Sara smiled, her eyes lighting up at the thought of Brian engaging in something new and interesting.

"Is it possible for the school counselor to spend some one-on-one time with Brian? Could she also try to find a personal counselor for him?" Leonard asked thoughtfully.

"I looked into finding a private counselor for Brian and his siblings, but there are huge waitlists," Lin shared.

"I'll talk to the school counselor, but I'm not sure she has the time to work with someone one-on-one,"

The Haunted Fire

Sara told them. "I'll also keep an eye out for any patterns or triggers in his behavior."

"If Brian decides he wants to spend some time with us on the job," Lin said, "we can all get together to discuss our observations and see if we can come up with some ideas to help Brian get back on track. I think Paul would be happy to have a group of people he can work with to help his brother."

"Sounds like a plan," Sara agreed, a glimmer of hope in her expression. "Thank you both so much. I knew I could count on you."

As they exchanged nods and smiles, for a moment, the idea of Paul being the arsonist ran through Lin's head and left her with a terrible sense of unease. If Paul were arrested for setting the fires, what would that do to Brian? It would be too terrible. The teen was already dealing with loss and chaos in his life.

Shaking herself from the thought, Lin took a deep breath and quickly pushed the ridiculous idea from her mind.

10

As the sun dipped low in the sky, the pretty light filtered through the lush hydrangeas and roses in Eleanor Hastings' garden. Lin took a deep breath, inhaling the mingling scents of the flowers. Eleanor's garden parties were always lovely, but this one held a tinge of melancholy since it was a fundraiser for the Hunter siblings. Lin sighed, thinking of Paul, Beth, and Brian left to fend for themselves since their father's gambling addiction had left them practically penniless.

Eleanor stood at the entrance to her enchanting flower garden, greeting guests with a warm, heartfelt smile. A banner hung above her, reading "Garden Party Fundraiser" in elegant golden letters. A wooden sign welcoming the guests was planted in the lawn under the banner to the side of the stone walkway.

"Welcome, Lin, Jeff," Mrs. Hastings said, extending her hand to the couple. "I'm so glad you could make it. The Hunters are truly grateful for your support."

"Of course, Eleanor," Lin replied, shaking her hand firmly. "We wouldn't miss it for the world." Beside her, Jeff nodded in agreement.

"Such a tragedy." Mrs. Hastings sighed, her gaze turning distant for a moment. "Both parents dying within a month of each other. Their father's gambling debts have left them in quite a bind, I'm afraid." She shook her head sadly. "And their poor mother... she fought her illness with everything she had, but in the end, it was just too much."

Lin felt a pang of sympathy. She knew all too well what it meant to lose one's parents, having experienced losing her father and mother in a car crash when she was little. And to be struggling financially on top of that? It was almost too much to deal with.

In the center of the garden, a small crowd had gathered around Paul, Beth, and Brian Hunter. Lin's heart ached at the sight of the three of them. The turnout was impressive, but they had a long way to go to raise the $100,000 the family of three so desperately needed.

She spotted Viv by the rose garden, handing an older woman a check. As Lin approached, she caught the end of their conversation. "...so tragic. The poor dears." The woman shook her head and wandered off into the crowd.

"Hey there." Lin hugged her cousin.

As they stepped further into the garden, Lin glanced around, taking in the lively scene before her. Guests chatted animatedly, sipping champagne and nibbling on hors d'oeuvres.

Viv turned with a sad smile. "I can't imagine being in the situation the Hunters are in."

"Have they raised much so far?" Lin asked, glancing around at the gardens.

"Nearly $75,000, but Eleanor's hoping to reach $100,000 by the end of the night." Viv tucked a stray hair behind her ear. "John and I gave a strong donation." Viv shared with her cousin what they'd donated. "It's the least we can do to help the family."

Lin nodded. "Jeff and I gave the same amount. I just hope it's all enough to reach the goal."

Eleanor tapped a spoon against her champagne flute, the crystal ringing like a bell in the warm evening air. The conversations faded as all eyes turned to her.

"Thank you all for coming this evening," she said. "As you know, the Hunter siblings recently lost both their mother and father. The purpose of tonight's fundraiser is to raise enough money to help these young people who have already endured so much. I hope that together, we can give them the fresh start they so desperately need."

Applause rippled through the crowd. Paul stepped forward, clutching a crumpled sheet of paper in his hands. "Thank you all for your kindness and generosity," he said, his voice hoarse. "After our parents died, we weren't sure how we were going to manage. We cannot express how grateful we are for your support." He swallowed hard, blinking back tears. "This means more to us than words can say."

Lin's eyes welled with tears. She glanced over at Viv, who was dabbing at her eyes with a tissue. Lin had grown up without her parents, but thankfully, she'd had her grandfather who had loved and cared for her.

The garden was awash with the silvery glow of twinkling lights and candle lanterns that illuminated the winding cobblestone paths. The sweet scent of honeysuckle and roses perfumed the air, and the savory aroma of food from the buffet tables smelled delicious.

A live band played softly in one corner near the house, the mellow strains of a jazz saxophone solo drifting through the crowd. Several couples swayed gently on the dance floor that had been set up over the grass, while others strolled along the garden paths or stood on the lawn, chatting and laughing.

Lin smiled, and for a moment, a sense of peace settled over her.

Despite the tragic circumstances that had brought them all there that night, there was a magical quality to the summer evening that filled her heart. The outpouring of love and support from Nantucket's close-knit community never ceased to amaze her.

"Penny for your thoughts?"

Lin glanced up to find Jeff looking down at her, his eyes glinting with warmth. She smiled, reaching up to smooth his tie. "Just feeling grateful we live in such a special place. And for family like Viv and John, and our good friends."

"I couldn't agree more," Jeff said. "This island has a way of bringing people together." His expression turned pensive. "Do you think the Hunters will stay on Nantucket now?"

"I hope so," Lin said, "but that will be up to them once they figure out their finances. All we can do is offer our support in any way we can." She gave his hand a gentle squeeze. "And make sure they know they're not alone."

Jeff nodded, his features softening. "That's why I love you, you know. Your heart is as big as the ocean."

Lin felt her cheeks turn pink. Even after a couple of years of marriage, Jeff's quiet affection still made her feel giddy.

"Thirsty?" he asked. "I was thinking of grabbing us glasses of champagne from the bar."

"Ooh, that would be nice, thank you." Lin gave him a playful swat on the arm. "Just don't be gone too long or I might have to send out a search party to find my favorite man."

Jeff chuckled, brushing a kiss against her forehead before making his way over to the bar.

Lin's gaze drifted to the lavish buffet tables, laden with artisanal cheeses, fresh-baked breads, locally sourced fruits and vegetables, and an assortment of tea sandwiches and quiches. The sweet aroma of chocolate cake and lemon tarts wafted through the air.

A shadow fell across the tables, and Lin glanced

up to find Michael Hansson, the Nantucket firefighter who was a friend of John's, approaching with a pleasant expression etched into his weathered features. He was slim, broad-shouldered, and had salt-and-pepper hair and blue eyes.

"Michael, it's good to see you," Lin greeted him with a smile. "How are you?"

"I'm doing okay." Michael's gaze drifted over the gathering. "Quite the turnout. The Hunter kids sure can use the help."

"It's horrible what they've gone through. I'm just glad the community has rallied around them."

Michael nodded, shoving a hand into the pocket of his jacket.

John, Viv, and Jeff came over to join them, and they spent a few minutes chatting about the event and island happenings.

"Any news on the fires?" John asked his friend.

"Afraid so. You all know to keep this confidential. In each case, the fire was started using Molotov cocktails—glass bottles filled with gasoline and a rag as a wick. We found one intact bottle at the scene of the latest fire. The arsonist is getting bolder and far more dangerous."

Michael's revelation stunned Lin into silence. She glanced around at the gathering, a sense of menace darkening the beauty of the evening. Could the arsonist be a guest at the garden party? Was he lurking among them? The thought made her shiver.

Taking a deep breath, Lin shook off her shudder, gazing out at the revelers with a wary eye. "Have there been any witnesses to the fires? Security camera footage? Anything that might help identify who's behind this?"

"A few neighbors have gotten glimpses of a slender man in dark clothing running away from the scenes," Michael said. "We've gathered some security films from homes in the areas of the fires. The footage is grainy, but analysts are reviewing it now, along with other evidence collected at the sites. Investigators are following up on a few leads, but so far, no definitive suspects," Michael explained, taking a sip of his drink. "The fires were started using a beer bottle filled with accelerant."

"Sounds like something out of a movie," Viv remarked, shaking her head. "How dangerous."

Michael replied gravely, "It's not just dangerous, it's lethal. We're lucky no one's been seriously hurt or killed yet."

John frowned, glancing around the garden party. "Do the police have any leads?" he asked, clearly troubled by the news.

"Nothing solid," Michael admitted, running a hand through his short, cropped hair, "but they're working night and day to find whoever's responsible."

Lin's mind raced with the implications of what Michael had just shared. She exchanged a worried glance with Jeff, feeling the weight of the situation settle heavily over them.

"Has there been any pattern to the fires?" Lin inquired, her voice barely above a whisper.

Michael hesitated for a moment, his eyes distant as he considered her question. "Not that anyone can tell," he finally answered, "but the fact that they've been started in such a specific way makes it clear that this isn't just some random act of vandalism. There's planning involved. We don't know if the houses are being specifically targeted."

"Let's hope they catch whoever's behind it soon," Viv murmured, her expression filled with concern.

As the friends mingled among the guests, they were drawn into conversations about the Hunter family and the fundraiser. It seemed that everyone had a story to share or a connection to the family, and the mood was both somber and hopeful.

"Such a tragedy," one woman murmured to Lin,

shaking her head sadly. "I knew their mother from church. She was a lovely person."

"Did you know that Paul is working hard to support his siblings?" another guest added, admiration shining in her eyes. "He's so determined to keep them together and provide for them."

As the conversation shifted back to the fundraiser and the guests continued to mingle, Lin felt a sense of unease. The knowledge of the arson fires and the unknown perpetrator added an undercurrent of danger to the otherwise peaceful evening.

"Have you noticed anyone acting strangely tonight?" Lin asked Viv, her eyes narrowing as she scanned the crowd.

Viv hesitated. "Not particularly. Why? Do you think our arsonist might be here?"

"Maybe," Lin admitted quietly, her heart racing at the thought. "It's worth keeping an eye out for anything out of the ordinary."

"I'll keep my eyes wide open." Viv nodded, her own gaze now scanning their fellow partygoers.

"Maybe we should split up," Jeff suggested, his hand resting protectively on the small of Lin's back. "We can cover more ground that way."

"Good idea," John agreed. "Viv and I will head

over toward the bar. You two check out the dance floor and buffet area."

As Lin and Jeff weaved through the throng of guests, she wondered if they might be in danger. Did the arsonist know she and Viv were looking into the fires? Could the arsonist be hiding among them?

As the night wore on, the guests continued to dance, laugh, and enjoy themselves, but a sense of unease had settled over Lin.

"Lin!" Viv called, rushing over with John in tow. "We found something!"

"Found what?" Lin asked, her stomach twisting into knots.

"Come see for yourself." The serious tone of John's voice sent a chill over Lin's skin.

John and Viv led Lin and Jeff to the entrance of the garden party where a wooden sign welcoming guests now bore a sinister message.

The word "BURN" was scratched into the sign, leaving no doubt that the arsonist had been there, watching them all along.

11

The next day, Viv adjusted the strap of her small purse on her shoulder as the breeze rustled the trees' leaves lining the main street of Nantucket's town center. She and Lin strolled side by side, their shoes occasionally clicking against the uneven ground.

"Three fires in one month," Viv said, her voice filled with concern.

Lin nodded as she scanned the quaint buildings and bustling shops that made up their quiet island home. "I know. The investigators don't seem to be any closer to arresting the arsonist, whoever it is," Lin murmured. "The firebug must have a reason for doing this, whether it's personal or some kind of twisted game."

Viv swallowed hard as her thoughts drifted to her beloved bookstore-café. What if it were targeted next? The mere idea sent a shiver down her back. She whispered, gripping her cousin's arm, "What if they come for my store?"

"Hey," Lin reassured her, giving her cousin's arm a comforting squeeze. "We'll figure this out. I know it's not much comfort, but the arsonist has only been targeting residential homes, not businesses. There are always people in town. The arsonist is choosing his targets carefully ... quiet streets, later at night."

"What if he targets my home?" Viv's eyes were wide.

The conversation was interrupted by the sudden sound of raised voices nearby. Both women glanced up to see a man shouting at the occupants of a car parked haphazardly in front of a small boutique. The man's face contorted in anger as he gestured wildly, clearly upset over the stolen parking spot.

"Should we...?" Viv hesitated, her eyes darting from the altercation to Lin.

"Let's just keep our distance," Lin suggested, watching the scene unfolding before them. "We don't want to get involved if it turns ugly."

"Right," Viv agreed, her grip on Lin's arm tightening as they continued to watch the heated exchange from a safe distance.

The man's shouts grew louder, echoing down the street and drawing the attention of passersby. Viv's heart pounded, her nerves frayed with anxiety over the fires and now this unexpected confrontation. It felt like their peaceful town was slowly unraveling at the seams. "Wait," she whispered, squinting at the irate man. "I think that's Michael Hansson."

"Michael? The firefighter?" Lin frowned, studying the man more closely. "You're right. What's he so upset about?"

"Let's find out." Viv took a step forward.

"Michael!" Lin called out, raising her hand in greeting.

The firefighter turned, surprise flickering across his face as he recognized the two women. Michael wiped the sweat off his brow, trying to regain his composure.

"Is everything okay?" Viv asked gently, searching the man's face. "We heard the commotion and wanted to make sure you were all right."

"Ah, yeah." Michael rubbed the back of his neck sheepishly. "Just a little disagreement over this parking spot."

Viv sensed Michael's discomfort. "We all have our bad days, right?"

"Tell me about it." Michael sighed, running a hand over his forehead. "Sorry for losing my temper," he said. "I just ... I got cut off by that car and it was the last straw."

"How are you holding up with work and all?" Lin asked gently, as she searched his face.

"Truth is," Michael hesitated, swallowing hard, "my wife and kids left me about a month ago. I've been trying to keep it together, but it's been tough." His voice cracked, and Viv could see the pain etched on his features, a stark contrast to the strong firefighter they knew he was.

"I'm so sorry." Viv reached out hesitantly to touch his arm. "John mentioned you and Wendy were having some problems. I'm sorry to hear it."

"Thanks," he replied quietly, forcing a tight smile. "I'll get through it, one way or another. I just need some time, I guess. I'm doing my best to stay focused on my job."

Lin nodded, her voice soft. "We should all get together some night, meet up at the pub where Viv and John play with their band. It would be nice to just hang out together."

"That's a good idea." Michael managed a weak

smile, his eyes reflecting the weariness that seemed to weigh him down. "I'd better do my errand and then head to work."

"Take care, Michael," Viv called out as they parted ways, feeling a heaviness form in her chest.

As the cousins continued down the street, the image of Michael's strained expression was in their minds. Something about their friend's behavior felt off — and they worried for him.

Lin couldn't ignore the nagging feeling that there was more going on beneath the surface. She glanced over at Viv, and with a low and cautious voice she asked, "Do you think ... no, never mind, it's too ridiculous."

"Go ahead," Viv encouraged, her heart pounding in anticipation of what her cousin might say. "What are you thinking?"

Lin sighed as she stared at the sidewalk beneath their feet. "It's just ... Michael's going through a lot right now, and it makes me wonder ... could he be connected to the fires?"

Viv's eyes widened in shock at the suggestion, but as much as she wanted to dismiss the idea, she knew she had to consider the possibility, however remote it might be. She felt ill at the thought that their friend could be capable of such a heinous crime. Biting her lip, she tried to push away the sick feeling in her stomach. "It's possible," she finally conceded, her voice barely above a whisper, "but it's just so hard to imagine."

"Believe me, I hope I'm wrong, too," Lin said. "I'm not saying he's the arsonist." She raised her hands in a helpless gesture. "I'm just ... thinking out loud. You and John know him better than I do, but we need to explore every angle, don't we?"

"Yes," Viv agreed, though her voice was tinged with uncertainty. "It's just so unbelievable to think Michael could do such a thing. He's a firefighter. He puts out fires; he doesn't start them."

Lin gave her cousin a sympathetic look. "Let's focus on our interview for now. We'll come back to Michael later if we need to."

Viv gave a reluctant nod.

Lin's body was tense as they resumed their walk down the main streets of Nantucket, almost sorry she'd brought up the idea that Michael might be behind the fires.

The afternoon sun beat down on them, but Viv felt cold inside, haunted by the thought that their friend might be harboring a dark secret.

Sunlight glinted off the shop windows along Nantucket's streets, casting dappled shadows on Viv and Lin as they walked side by side. The scent of saltwater and fresh-baked pastries mingled in the warm air but did little to lessen the gnawing unease that plagued both women.

As they walked on, the laughter of tourists and the bustle of town felt strangely distant, as if Viv and Lin had been transported to another place - one filled with secrets and the ever-present threat of fire. Their footsteps marked time like a slow-burning fuse.

∼

As they approached the lovely antique house, they admired the beautiful landscaping around the home.

"Is the Higgins family one of your and Leonard's clients?" Viv asked as her eyes wandered over the flower garden behind the white picket fence.

"They aren't." Lin shook her head. "I might need to plug our landscaping business while we're here though."

Viv chuckled and kidded her cousin, "You should have brought one of your business pamphlets to give them."

When they rang the front doorbell, a middle-aged woman opened the door and greeted them. Flora Worthington Higgins had short, light brown hair and big brown eyes. She wore a colorful summer dress and sandals. "Do come in. How nice to meet you." The woman led the way to the back of the house and into a family room with huge windows on three sides.

An older woman with stylishly-cut white hair sat in a comfortable easy chair by one of the windows.

Flora said, "This is my mother, Elizabeth."

The young women shook hands with the matriarch, and Elizabeth greeted them warmly.

"Please, have a seat." Flora gestured toward two white armchairs, her eyes never leaving their faces. "I understand you have some questions about our family's ... history."

Elizabeth spoke up with a smile. "Everyone knows Arthur Radcliffe was a criminal and a scoundrel. Over the decades, the family has tried to do all we can to convince people that Arthur was an aberration and did not represent what our family stands for."

"We know about the crimes he committed," Flora told them. "It's shameful to have someone like that as an ancestor, but we do all we can to do good

... with our time as well as our money. What we can tell you about him?"

Lin cleared her throat, trying to repress the urge to glance over her shoulder as though expecting to find ghosts lurking in every corner. "We're concerned about the series of fires that have occurred recently on the island. We're also students of history and wondered if you might be able to shed some light on any... similarities between these incidents and those of your ancestor."

Elizabeth replied, "Ask us your questions, and we shall do our best to answer them."

Flora walked over to a large desk in a corner of the room. "We have albums with old newspaper clippings, documents, and letters that you might like to see." She carried them over to a round glass table and spread them out so Lin and Viv could look them over.

When Lin glanced out the window, she had to stifle a gasp. Her ghost stood outside on the lawn, staring in at her with a somber expression that sent a chill over her skin.

"Lin?" Viv asked.

Turning her head and blinking, she looked at her cousin. "I didn't hear what you said."

"This letter is Arthur Radcliffe's confession."

Lin's eyes went wide. "He confessed? To setting the fire?"

"No, he isn't the one who set it," Flora said. "Arthur hired a young man to set it for him."

"Why?" Lin was dumbfounded.

"To try to evade arrest," Elizabeth said from her chair across the room. "He couldn't even commit a crime properly. Arthur thought he could buy whatever it was he wanted. He convinced a teenage boy to set it and then let the boy take the fall for the crime. Eventually, when the authorities were on to him, Arthur made a confession. Of course, because the man was a weasel, he was cagey about his involvement saying that the teenager didn't follow directions and that was the reason the fire got out of control and killed the family who lived there. Arthur said it wasn't his fault. It certainly was his fault. His actions killed a family, as well as a young boy, Nathan Post, who was desperate and poor. Arthur served time in prison which was exactly what he deserved. I'm ashamed to say I'm the man's descendant."

"What happened to the boy?" Lin asked.

"The boy," Flora told them, "died in prison after serving only one year of his sentence." The woman sighed. "The boy was destitute. His mother was penniless. He wanted the money Arthur paid him to pay for food for his mother and sister. Arthur took advantage of the teen to get what he wanted. He was a poor excuse for a human being."

Elizabeth spoke again. "Arthur blamed William Johnson, the man who died in the fire with his family, for his financial woes. A business associate of Arthur's debunked that notion. Arthur lost his fortune because he made poor investments and decisions. The loss of his money was all Arthur's fault. William Johnson had nothing to do with it. In fact, Mr. Johnson tried to help Arthur out of his troubles, but Arthur refused."

"What a mess," Viv whispered.

"What a terrible story." Lin looked out the window to the rear yard, but the ghost was gone.

After another hour of looking at the documents, Lin thanked the women for their time before she and Viv stepped back outside.

As they walked away from the house, the echoes of their footsteps mingled with the cries of seagulls overhead. Lin felt like they were leaving one ghost-filled realm only to enter another, and although they now had a clearer understanding of the past, the identity of the present-day arsonist remained as elusive and dangerous as ever.

12

In the dark night, the moon hid behind a veil of clouds over the quaint Nantucket neighborhood. Jeff was sleeping soundly in their bedroom, but Lin couldn't sleep and had gone to the kitchen to make some tea. Glancing out the window, she rubbed her eyes and blinked fast several times to clear her vision. She saw a faint, shimmering light out on the deck. She felt a cool shiver run over her arms, knowing that William Johnson had returned.

Stepping outside, Lin approached the spectral figure, his ethereal form flickering like a candle struggling to stay lit. The air was still, and the only sounds that broke the silence were the squeak of branches swaying in the gentle night breeze.

After visiting the descendants of Arthur

Radcliffe, Lin had come to the conclusion that William had known all along who was responsible for his and his family's deaths in the house fire more than a century ago ... and that it wasn't what he'd wanted Lin to find out.

"William," Lin said softly, trying to keep her voice steady. "I understand now that you knew who was responsible for the fire that killed you and your family, and I know that wasn't what you wanted me to focus on." She knew that there had to be more than simply discovering who the arsonist was, but what could it be? If he wasn't trying to reveal the identity of his own murderer, then what could be so important that he had reached out from beyond the grave? Lin knew there had to be more to it than that.

"William," she whispered into the still night air. "Why are you so concerned about these recent fires? What do you want my help with?"

The ghost stared at her, unable to speak, his eyes filled with a depth of sadness that tore at her heart. He raised a translucent hand as if to reach out to her, but it wavered and fell back to his side ... the barrier between life and death seemed too great.

Frustration welled in Lin; she could feel the answer just beyond her grasp. Her voice cracked with emotion. "Help me understand. I know you want the arsonist found, but why is this important to you? You died over a hundred years ago. What am I missing?"

William's eyes bore into hers, desperation and sorrow intermingling in his ghostly gaze. He tried once more to gesture, but it was futile. Lin's heart ached with the knowledge that she couldn't decipher his silent request for help.

As she searched his translucent features for any clue, a sudden realization struck her. "You're trying to protect someone, aren't you?" Lin asked, her pulse quickening. "Someone who's still alive - someone who needs your help."

William's eyes seemed to light up, and for a fleeting moment, Lin thought she saw a glimmer of hope in them.

"Okay," Lin said, determination running through her. "I'll do everything I can to find this person and I'll try to keep them safe, but I need your help, too. Show me whatever signs you can to guide me in the right direction."

The ghostly figure nodded solemnly, his particles swirling faster and faster as he began to fade away. Before completely disappearing, Lin caught a glimpse of what looked like gratitude in his eyes.

It was up to her to untangle the web of secrets.

She would protect the living and honor the dead - she owed it to William and his tragic past.

With that, she stepped back into the warmth and safety of her home, determined to figure out the mystery of her ghost.

∼

The next evening, the two cousins walked into Smitty's Place, the dimly lit bar buzzing with conversation and laughter. The familiar scent of beer and peanuts filled the air as they approached the bartender, who recognized them from their previous visit.

"Ah, it's you two again," he said, nodding toward Lin and Viv. "You were asking about that anxious guy, right? The one who was fiddling with the matches. Turns out he's here tonight."

Lin exclaimed in surprise, "He's here?"

"Over there."Tthe bartender pointed to a corner table where a young man sat alone, sipping a drink.

"It's Paul Hunter." Viv's eyes widened in surprise.

"Thanks," Lin said to the bartender, and she and Viv made their way to Paul's table.

"Hey, there. Mind if we join you for a few

minutes?" Viv asked with a friendly smile as they reached the table.

"Oh, hey." Paul shifted uncomfortably in his seat. "Please, pull up some chairs."

"Thanks," Lin said as she and Viv settled down. "How are you?"

"Doing okay." The tone of Paul's voice said otherwise.

"The garden party fundraiser was a great time," Viv told him. "We hope it was a help to you and your siblings."

"Definitely," Paul agreed, rubbing his eyes. "It means a lot to Beth, Brian, and me. You know we've been struggling."

"It must be tough managing everything on your own," Viv empathized.

"Tell me about it." Paul sighed, taking another sip of his drink. "I never knew Dad had such a terrible gambling problem. Now I'm responsible for my siblings and trying to sort out this financial mess."

"I'm sorry you're going through this," Lin offered.

"I appreciate that," he replied quickly, wiping his palms on his jeans. "There's a lot on my plate right now. Sometimes I come here for a beer just to sit quietly and get away from everything for a little while."

"It's good to take some time for yourself," Viv said, exchanging a concerned glance with Lin. "We just wanted to say hi. We'll let you get back to your evening."

"Thanks," Paul mumbled, offering a weak smile as Lin and Viv left the table.

After having a drink at the bar, Lin and Viv stepped out of Smitty's Place. The chilly night air moved gently over their skin.

The image of Paul's anxious expression was at the front of Lin's mind, and she wondered about the young man and how he was handling all the stress in his life. His anxiety, combined with the pressure of managing his family's affairs and dealing with his girlfriend leaving him could have driven him to act out in an extreme way. She glanced around nervously, as if expecting William's ghost to appear at any moment.

"Viv," Lin whispered, her voice heavy with uncertainty. "Could Paul be the arsonist? He's having such a hard time. His problems could have pushed him to do something awful."

"Maybe," Viv conceded, her brow furrowed in thought. "I have to admit I was thinking the same thing, but we need more evidence. We're just speculating. For now, we have to keep digging."

Lin nodded, her eyes drifting upwards to the inky black sky. A sea of stars twinkled in the darkness, and for a brief moment, she found comfort in their beauty, but as her thoughts returned to the mysterious arson cases and her ghost, her mood darkened once again. "Want to come to my house for tea?" Lin suggested, breaking the silence. "We need a plan."

"Yeah. Tea would be nice," Viv replied, linking arms with her cousin. Together, they walked towards Lin's house, their footsteps echoing on the sidewalk.

As they approached the front door, Lin felt an odd sensation - like someone was watching them. She glanced over her shoulder, half-expecting to see William's shimmering light again, but there was no one there.

"I've been thinking," Lin began hesitantly as they stepped inside, "about what William wants us to find out. He knew who killed him and his family and he wants our help to stop the arsonist, but I think there's something more to it."

"That could be," Viv mused, looking thoughtful, "or it could be something else entirely. We just don't have enough information yet. Let's have some tea and talk strategy."

"Good idea," Lin agreed. As the kettle heated up,

her thoughts swirled like the steam rising from its spout. What was the connection between William's tragic past and the present-day arsonist?

"Is it even possible Paul could be the person behind the fires?" Viv took mugs from the cabinet.

"Emotional upheaval can cause all kinds of behaviors," Lin pointed out, "some harmless and others not so much."

"Paul definitely has had tremendous emotional upheaval. His parents died and he's been left to care for his siblings and try to straighten out a financial mess. It could push anyone over the edge."

"And what about Michael Hansson?" Lin poured hot water into the mugs.

Viv sighed. "I recall reading about a firefighter who was a captain and arson investigator who started setting fires in the area where he lived. He's believed to have set over two thousand fires."

"I remember that story. What was his motivation?" Lin asked.

"I don't think one was ever given. I don't know if he had some sort of crisis or terrible stress in his life, but for some unknown reason, he turned to setting fires."

"Some things are unexplainable." Lin set a pot of cream next to the tea mugs.

As they sipped their tea and discussed their next steps, Lin knew there was more to her ghost's story. With each unanswered question, the mystery only deepened - and Lin knew they had to keep pushing or someone was going to get hurt ... and soon.

13

The young woman navigated the quaint Nantucket streets with Nicky trotting next to her. Lin, with her hair pulled back into a ponytail, walked at a brisk pace toward Viv's house for dinner. Jeff and John were working late so the cousins decided to eat on Viv's deck and enjoy the evening together. Lin was eager to spend some quiet time relaxing with Viv.

As Lin and the dog turned the corner into her cousin's neighborhood, she glanced at the burned house just a few doors up from her destination. The home's blackened walls caused her heart to beat a little faster, and she felt a chill in the air despite the warmth of the late May evening.

The scent of charred wood and smoke still lingered even though the fire had been extinguished days before. It was an unsettling reminder of how quickly tragedy could strike in their small island community. As Lin moved closer, she saw that the once vibrant garden surrounding the home was now suffocated by ash and soot.

From across the street, she paused for a moment, studying the wreckage. The skeletal remains of the house stood like a dark sentinel against the peaceful backdrop of the setting sun. Windows stared back at her, shattered and empty, as if the house itself were mourning its loss. The jagged remnants of the roof jutted out at odd angles, evidence of the raging inferno that had consumed it.

Her heart sank as she tried to shake off the heaviness of the scene. Lin breathed in deeply, attempting to focus on enjoying a nice evening with Viv. Just as she was about to head toward her cousin's house, movement caught her eye and she spotted a slender man standing near the burned house, seemingly absorbed in examining the charred remains. Intrigued, she paused and watched him from where she and Nicky stood across the street.

The man appeared to be in his late thirties or early forties. He had sharp cheekbones and his ash-blond hair fell across his forehead, partially obscuring his eyes. He wore a long, dark sweater that seemed out of place on such a warm evening. His posture seemed tense with his hands buried deep in his pockets, weight shifting uneasily from one foot to the other, as though he could not decide whether he should stay or go.

Why would someone be so engrossed in the burned ruins of a house? Maybe he was a journalist looking to document the aftermath of the fire for a news story, or maybe he was a neighbor, mourning the loss of his friends' house ... although Lin didn't think she'd ever seen him before.

As she watched, she noticed that the man would occasionally glance around as if checking to make sure no one was watching him. His demeanor suggested something more than mere journalistic interest or neighborly concern.

Her thoughts raced, and as she continued to observe him from a distance, she felt a growing sense of unease. Was it her imagination or did he seem to be scrutinizing the burned house with an almost obsessive intensity?

The questions swirled through Lin's mind as she stood there, rooted to the spot by her growing apprehension. Taking a deep breath, she stepped off the sidewalk and crossed the road.

"Excuse me," Lin called out hesitantly.

The slender man's head snapped in her direction. His eyes, a piercing blue, widened in surprise. He blinked rapidly before regaining his composure, his thin lips pressed into a tight line.

"Yes?" he asked, his tone guarded and aloof.

"Um, hi," Lin stammered, feeling her cheeks flush with embarrassment. "I live nearby, and I couldn't help notice you looking at the house."

"Oh. I'm not causing any trouble, am I?" he replied, rubbing the back of his neck. His gaze never left hers, making her feel a little unnerved by his laser beam attention.

"No, no, not at all," Lin assured him, trying to sound friendly. "I was just wondering what brings you here. Are you visiting Nantucket?"

"I suppose you could say that," he said, his voice smooth and measured yet tinged with an unidentifiable accent. "I'm just passing through town. I heard about the fire and thought I'd take a look."

Lin's eyes narrowed as she studied his face, searching for any hint of deception, but his expression remained impassive.

"It's a shame, isn't it?" she commented, attempting to keep the conversation going. "Do you know the people who lived here?"

The Haunted Fire

"No, I don't," he admitted, shaking his head, "but I am familiar with tragedies like this one."

"Really?" Lin inquired, her curiosity piqued. "Are you an investigator of some kind?"

"Something like that," he responded cryptically, a vague smile playing at the corner of his mouth.

"Interesting," Lin mused, her mind racing with possibilities. Was he here to help work the arson case, or was there another reason for his interest in the damaged house?

"Will you be on-island for the summer?"

"No, not that long."

"Can I ask you something?" Lin said hesitantly, her curiosity getting the better of her. "Why are you so interested in the fire."

The man's gaze remained fixed on the burned house as if his thoughts were worlds away. After a brief moment of silence, he turned his attention back to Lin. "I've seen many things in my life," he replied softly. "I've learned that tragedies like these often hold secrets that need to be uncovered, secrets that could help prevent future disasters."

Lin raised an eyebrow, confused by what he'd said. What was his role in uncovering secrets? She took a deep breath, trying to steady her nerves and maintain her composure as she considered his cryptic response. She knew she should probably leave it at that and continue on her way to Viv's house, but she wanted to ask the stranger a few more questions.

"Have you been hired by the town to look into the fires?"

"I don't have a professional interest in the events."

"Would you mind if I asked your name?" Lin ventured, hoping to establish a more personal connection with the man.

"Of course not," he replied, his eyes meeting hers with an intensity that made her shiver. "I'm Ethan Bagshaw."

"Nice to meet you. I'm Lin," she said, offering a tentative smile. Inside, her thoughts raced like wildfire. Could this man be the arsonist?

Ethan's eyes suddenly flicked away, and he appeared to be studying the charred remains of the house with renewed interest. His fingers drummed nervously on his thigh, and when he finally spoke again, his voice had taken on a hesitant quality.

"Actually," Ethan began, still not looking at her, "I've been researching fires and their causes for some time now. It's ... a bit of a hobby, I suppose."

Lin watched his face closely as he continued to

avoid eye contact with her. She glanced back at the scorched facade, noting how the fire had spread unnaturally quickly through the structure. She glanced at Ethan out of the corner of her eye. Could Ethan be more than just a curious bystander?

Her heart pounded hard. It certainly wasn't unheard of for an arsonist to return to the scene of their crime. Lin had also learned that sometimes those responsible couldn't resist observing their handiwork firsthand.

"Have you found anything ... interesting about this house fire?" she asked cautiously, trying to keep her tone neutral and unassuming.

"Well, every fire has its own story to tell," Ethan said. "Some are tragic accidents, while others..." He trailed off, leaving the implication hanging in the air between them.

If he were indeed the arsonist, what was his end game? Was he merely seeking validation for his actions, or was there a deeper motivation for him to be standing there?

"What do you mean ... others?" she prompted.

"Others," Ethan replied slowly, his eyes narrowing as if gauging her reaction, "aren't accidents. They're the result of something far more sinister."

Lin drew on her ability to read people, searching for any subtle cues or giveaways that might reveal more about the man. "Have you been following the investigation closely?" she asked.

"Only as much as anyone else," Ethan replied, shrugging nonchalantly. "I've always found fire to be such a fascinating element. So destructive, yet so captivating."

His words struck a nerve with Lin. There was something about the way he spoke, the almost reverent tone he used when describing the fire that set off alarm bells in her mind.

"Captivating?" she echoed, trying to keep her voice steady. "I suppose, in a way, but it's also terrifying, especially when it's used as a weapon."

"Ah, yes," Ethan agreed, his smile never faltering. "Therein lies the true allure of fire – its ability to both create and destroy, all at the whim of its wielder."

After a few moments of silence between them, Lin said, "Well, I'd better get going. I'm meeting someone for dinner. It was nice talking with you. I hope you enjoy your visit."

"Thank you," he replied, his voice taking on a soft tone.

As Lin turned to leave, she cast a glance over her

shoulder. The slender man was still standing there, staring at the charred remains of the house, a strange mixture of fascination and sorrow etched into his features.

Something about the encounter felt off. The evasive answers, the intense interest in the house fire, calling the fire captivating ... was that enough to suspect him? Was he just an oddball with an unusual interest in fires? Was she simply letting her imagination run wild?

As she and her dog walked toward Viv's house, she saw her cousin in the front garden and waved at her.

Viv said, "There you are. Dinner is ready and waiting." She bent to pat Nicky while he squirmed and wiggled in delight.

"Sorry," Lin said, forcing a smile. "I got a bit ... sidetracked."

"By what?" Viv asked, curious.

"Just ... a tourist."

"Ah, well, they do tend to wander around here," Viv kidded as she led Lin and Nicky to the front door. "Come on, let's go inside."

The house smelled of lasagna; the scent of onions, basil, cheeses, and tomato sauce making Lin's stomach growl. The women carried the salad, the glasses and a bottle of wine, and the freshly-baked lasagna out to the deck, as Nicky and Viv's cat Queenie raced out into the yard. Viv had set the table earlier with light pink plates, silverware, napkins, and candles. The string lights sparkled overhead as the cousins sat down to eat.

"That tourist I mentioned? He was really odd." Lin scooped salad onto her plate.

Viv looked straight at Lin. "Odd? Odd, how?"

"He was intensely interested in the house fire. He was just standing there staring at the burned house. I talked to him. He called fire captivating."

"That's a strange word to describe arson." Viv's eyes narrowed as she sipped from her wine glass.

Lin said, "I wondered if he was the arsonist, come back to admire his handiwork."

"Is he a native?"

"He said he was here visiting the island. He was kind of evasive about it. His name is Ethan Bagshaw, but I suppose he could have been lying about that." Lin sprinkled some grated cheese over her square of lasagna. "This smells delicious. I'm starving."

"Did he say where he was from?" Viv questioned.

"I didn't ask and he didn't say. I guess I could pass the information on to Michael Hansson. He could share it with the fire investigators if he thought it was important."

"Michael. The firefighter." Viv rolled her eyes. "Another suspect in the arson case."

Lin looked out over the yard watching the dog and cat playfully chase each other around the trees. She wished her life could be as simple and sweet as theirs was.

14

It was a warm, humid day when Lin, Jeff, Viv, and John strolled through the bustling church farmer's market and June festival. As Lin watched a clown do magic tricks, she smiled when Viv's laughter twinkled like wind chimes.

Firefighter Michael Hansson came over and greeted them. "A great turnout."

"It sure is," John remarked. "I think the crowds are even bigger than last year."

Michael looked at Lin. "I passed your information to the investigators about the man who seemed too interested in the latest house fire. I didn't think they'd do anything with the tip, but I was wrong. They checked ferry and plane records for the man's name and discovered he wasn't on-island when any of the fires were set."

Even though she knew it was a long shot, Lin was disappointed at the news. "He was an unusual person. I'm glad they checked him out and eliminated him as a suspect."

They chatted a little longer with Michael before he left them to meet up with a friend.

"Hey, look. The Hunter siblings are over there," Lin remarked, gesturing towards the young trio managing a stand brimming with fresh produce from a nearby farm. "They must be volunteering here today."

"Let's go say hi," Jeff suggested, his hand reaching for Lin's as they navigated through the crowd together with John and Viv following close behind.

"Hi, Brian, Amy, and Paul," Lin greeted them warmly. "How are you guys doing? You're working the farm stand today?"

"Hey, Lin. Hi, everybody," Paul responded, forcing a smile that didn't quite reach his eyes. "We're doing all right, considering everything, I guess."

"The vegetables look amazing," John chimed in, trying to keep the conversation light. He picked up a ripe tomato and admired its vibrant red hue.

"They really do," Beth replied, her voice soft. "We

decided to volunteer today, and they assigned us here for the morning. Mom volunteered every year. The church community was important to her."

As they chatted amiably, Lin noticed Brian's hands clenched into fists when a customer accidentally dropped a couple of ears of corn to the ground. The young teen's face reddened, and he snapped, "Can't you be more careful?!"

"Brian, it's okay," Paul interjected calmly, already bending down to help collect the runaway corn.

Lin exchanged a concerned glance with Viv, who gave a slight nod. They both knew that losing one's parents was an earth-shattering experience, and the stress of having their lives upended was taking its toll on all the Hunters, especially Brian.

"Sorry about that," Brian muttered, trying to regain his composure as he bagged the vegetables for the flustered customer. "I didn't mean to snap."

"Hey, it's okay. You apologized, and that's what matters," Lin reassured him gently, placing a comforting hand on his shoulder.

As the conversation carried on, Lin kept an eye on Brian, his outburst lingering in the back of her mind. She stood beside Viv, watching the people strolling through the festival on the church grounds. Children with painted faces darted between stalls, their laughter mixing with the notes of a fiddler playing nearby. A waft of freshly baked bread and sweet apple cider filled the air, but despite the happy atmosphere, Lin's thoughts remained on the Hunter siblings, the lingering weight of their recent grief heavy in her chest.

"Hey, Paul," Lin said to the young man, catching his attention from across the table where he was arranging a tray of broccoli and carrots. "I couldn't help notice your fingers. What happened there?"

Paul looked down at his bandaged fingers, flexing them slightly before turning back to Lin with a rueful smile. "Oh, that? I was trying to save a plate of marshmallows from falling into a fire pit last night, but I wasn't quite fast enough. Just a few burns, nothing serious."

"Ouch." Viv winced sympathetically, glancing over at her cousin.

Was that really how Paul burned his fingers or was there another reason? Lin wondered. "Sounds painful, but at least it wasn't worse."

"Very true." Paul nodded.

As the conversation continued, Lin had the feeling that something was amiss. She glanced around at the event's activities expecting to see her ghost, but he wasn't there.

"Lin?" Viv's voice broke through her cousin's distraction, pulling her back to the present moment. "Why are you spacing out?"

"Sorry, I just..." Lin hesitated, biting her lip as she tried to articulate her thoughts. "It's hard sometimes, you know? Knowing what I can see, and not wanting to suspect people who may not be guilty."

"Your gift is both a blessing and a curse," Viv acknowledged, her voice soft and understanding. "But remember, it's important to trust your instincts. If something feels off, there's usually a reason for it."

"Thanks." Lin took a deep breath as she tried to let go of her doubts. "I just hope we can make some progress on this case. It feels like we've been stuck in quicksand lately."

"I know," Viv agreed, giving Lin's hand a reassuring squeeze.

As the festival continued to buzz with activity, Lin knew that she needed to keep searching for answers – and that meant staying vigilant and trusting her intuition, no matter where it led her.

Stopping at a food truck selling coffee and pastries, Lin, Jeff, Viv, and John joined the line, and in a few moments, Brian, Paul, and Beth came over to stand behind them.

"This truck has the best coffee," Beth said.

"And the donuts are great." Brian smiled, looking eagerly at the truck.

"I know. I love this truck," Viv agreed.

"Sorry if we seem a bit ... off today," Paul quietly confessed to Lin, rubbing at the bandages on his fingers. "Things have been pretty tough for us lately. There's a lot going on."

"Are you okay?" Lin asked gently, her voice filled with genuine concern.

"Everyone knows we're in a financial mess," Paul admitted, his voice tight with frustration. "We've been thinking about selling our home and moving to the mainland, where things are less expensive."

"That would be a big change for all of you," Jeff pointed out.

"And Paul just started a new job as a mechanical engineer," Beth added, a note of sadness in her voice. "It would be too bad if he had to quit and look for something else."

Paul nodded. "It's a great job, but we might have to leave if we can't sort out our finances."

"I'm so sorry to hear about your troubles," Jeff said sympathetically. "I can't imagine how difficult it must be for you."

Paul's eyes shifted uncomfortably as he avoided

the man's gaze. "We're just trying to take it one day at a time, you know?"

"Of course," Lin said quietly, her heart aching for the siblings even as her intuition continued to nag at her. She looked at Paul's fingers. Did he really get burned at a fire pit? Could he be the one who set the fires? The question echoed through her mind, but she forced herself to focus on the conversation at hand.

"Have you contacted my financial advisor?" Viv asked, her voice gentle yet practical. "She could help you come up with a plan to manage your expenses and maybe even find a way to stay on the island."

Lin chimed in, "It might be worth exploring all your options before making such a big decision."

"Maybe," Paul said hesitantly, rubbing at the burn marks on his fingers, "but I'm not sure we can afford that kind of help. I never called your advisor," he told Viv. "I know we can't afford her."

"Actually," Viv said, her face brightening, "I think Heather, Leonard's girlfriend, knows someone who specializes in financial planning. She often will offer a reduced fee or even work pro bono."

"Really?" Beth asked, hope flickering in her eyes. "That would be amazing."

Lin nodded, her heart swelling with warmth at

Viv's suggestion. "We'll talk to Heather and she can connect you with her friend."

"Thank you so much," Brian interjected, his earlier burst of annoyance at a customer seemingly forgotten. "I really don't want to move."

As they parted ways with the Hunters, Lin glanced around at the bustling festival, taking in the sights and sounds of the various vendors and performers entertaining the crowd. A group of children giggled as they chased each other around the trees, while nearby, a juggler tossed balls into the air, drawing gasps of amazement from the onlookers.

"Are you really okay?" Viv asked, noticing her cousin's distraction. "You seem a bit ... on edge."

"Sorry," Lin murmured, reining in her wandering thoughts. "I'm just trying to make sure we don't overlook anything important."

"What do you make of Paul's burned fingers?" Viv kept her voice down.

"Seeing them gave me a cold chill." Lin sighed. "I can't stand the idea that we have to be suspicious of Paul."

"There haven't been any new fires recently though, so he must have burned his fingers the way he said he did," Viv suggested.

"Unless he burned them making new Molotov

cocktails for the next fire." Lin frowned. "It can't be him, can it?"

Viv didn't reply right away, but when she finally spoke, her voice was heavy with worry. "I sure hope not."

Lin could only pray that her instincts were wrong – that Paul Hunter was an innocent victim of circumstance and not the perpetrator of the recent arson cases.

15

The dimly lit pub hummed with chatter as the patrons eagerly awaited Viv and John's popular band to take the stage. Lin, her brown hair cascading over her shoulders in long waves, nervously tapped her fingers on the wooden table near the stage where she sat with her husband Jeff, Leonard, and Heather. The candles flickered in the center of their table as they discussed the recent string of house fires.

"Three houses in such a short time," Lin mused, her eyes clouded with concern. "I can't help but worry about what's next."

"Everyone's on edge," Leonard agreed. "It seems this arsonist is growing bolder with each fire."

Heather, who didn't know anything about Lin's ghost-seeing abilities, shook her head. "I've been talking to some colleagues about it. Everyone's nervous, and the investigators don't seem to have any solid leads yet."

Jeff leaned forward, resting his elbows on the table. "We just have to hope they catch him soon."

Lin sensed the conversation was making their unease worse, so she decided to change the subject. "Leonard and I have been making good progress on the English gardens we're creating for a new client. It's really coming together beautifully."

"Yeah," Leonard brightened at the opportunity to discuss their work. "We've been mixing traditional and modern elements for a really unique look. Yesterday, we installed a fancy rose arbor that will be the entrance to the garden."

"I love that idea," Heather exclaimed, a smile lighting up her face.

Leonard beamed at her. "We've been choosing plants for color and fragrance, but ones that will attract bees and butterflies, too. We'd do that anyway, but it was important to the clients."

Jeff turned to his wife. "That sounds amazing."

Lin nodded. "I haven't been able to tell you much about the gardens because we've both been so busy lately. I've always loved the idea of creating spaces that look beautiful but are beneficial to the environment. It's always a fun challenge."

As they continued to discuss the details of the English garden project, Lin's thoughts drifted back to the arsonist. She knew she should focus on the present moment and enjoy the company of her friends, but the unknown perpetrator's actions weighed heavily on her mind.

The pub came alive when Viv and John's band took the stage and started the set, filling the air with electric energy. The crowd began to sway and dance, drawn into the infectious rhythm of the music. Lin tapped her foot in time to the beat, feeling a smile spread across her face.

"Wow, they're really good tonight," Jeff shouted over the music, leaning closer to Lin so she could hear him.

"Definitely," Lin agreed as she watched the band members perform on the stage. She reached for Jeff's hand and pulled him onto the small dance floor, where they had a great time dancing together. When the set was over, they headed back to the table and sat.

"Some pretty good moves out there," Leonard told them.

"Why didn't you join us?" Lin asked.

"I tried to get him out there, but he wouldn't budge." Heather took a sip from her beer mug.

"Don't be an old stick-in-the-mud," Lin chided her business partner.

"I only have so much energy, and I used it all up working in the hot sun today," Leonard informed her. "Maybe you should have done a little more of the work on the gardens so I'd have the pep to dance tonight."

"Don't pull that argument. It isn't going to work on me." Lin gently elbowed the man.

The group's conversation shifted as Heather shared news about a recent phone call with Paul Hunter. "I spoke to Paul earlier today," she began, raising her voice to be heard over the music. "I've been trying to set him up with a financial planner to help him and his siblings make the right choices."

"A real tragedy," Leonard commented, shaking his head, "to lose both parents so suddenly and to be left with so little."

"Thanks for doing this for them," Lin told Heather.

Heather nodded solemnly. "It's hard enough for young people to find their footing in today's world without having to deal with this kind of grief and responsibility."

"Have you found someone who can help them?" Lin asked.

"Still working on it," Heather admitted. "I've been calling around, trying to find a planner who specializes in cases like theirs. I want someone who will give them a good price for the service. I think I have someone. She's excellent and wants to help them. She might even do it for free."

"Good for you," Jeff chimed in, admiration shining in his eyes. "It will really make a difference for that family."

"Paul actually said something a little shocking," Heather admitted, her voice low as she leaned in closer to be heard above the music. "He told me he wishes the arsonist would burn down his house so he could collect the insurance money and move with his siblings to the mainland."

Lin's eyes widened, and she felt a chill run down her back despite the warmth of the crowded room. Jeff's hand tightened around his pint glass.

"Are you serious?" Lin asked, disbelief coloring her tone. "That's ... that's just crazy."

"I reminded him, in a gentle way, just how dangerous and insensitive that statement was," Heather continued, her expression tinged with disapproval. "He was apologetic when he realized how it sounded. There are innocent people who have had their homes destroyed by those fires, and I was initially surprised that he could even think about saying something like that, but I know Paul is under terrible stress." She shrugged.

Leonard said, stroking his chin thoughtfully, "It does make you wonder. I hate to say it, but could Paul be the arsonist? Desperation can drive people to do terrible things."

The table went silent for a moment, each of them lost in their own thoughts. Even the lively music seemed to recede into the background.

Her gaze flitting between her friends, Lin finally said, "He's grieving, he's exhausted, and he's overwhelmed. Could he really be capable of such a thing?"

Heather said firmly, "We'll find him the help he needs, but I made it very clear that joking or not, there are some things you simply don't say."

"Right," Jeff agreed, taking a long swig of his beer. "Let's just hope the investigators can put an end to all this soon. For everyone's sake."

As the band struck up a new song, Lin felt a growing sense of unease. Her thoughts were heavy with concern for Paul and his siblings. The music that had been a happy distraction, now just seemed like a soundtrack to their grim speculations. She knew they had to find the arsonist and bring the ghost peace, but as the night wore on, she felt that the fire was closing in—and their time was running out.

Jeff placed his hand over Lin's. "You're worried about Paul, aren't you?"

Lin hesitated, glancing at Leonard and Heather before nodding. "I am. He's so young. The burden of caring for his siblings and the financial worries ... it must be crushing him."

"Sometimes, people say things they don't really mean when they're under pressure," Leonard offered, his gaze thoughtful as he swirled the ice in his drink.

Lin's fingers tapped an anxious rhythm against the table. "But it's not just about what he said. It's about everything he's going through—the turmoil, the responsibility. I wish there was someone who could help them, but they're all alone in this. They don't have any other relatives."

Heather frowned as she took a slow sip from her glass. "There must be something we can do. We can't just sit by and watch him suffer like this."

"Or even just offer a listening ear," Leonard added, his expression softening. "Sometimes, that's all people need—a friend who'll be there for them."

Lin sighed and her eyes locked on the flickering candle at the center of the table. "I hope we can do something—anything—to help ease his burden. We can't change what's happened, but maybe we can make the path forward a little easier for him, Beth, and Brian. We brought it up with him a couple of weeks ago, but I'll talk to him again about seeing someone."

As Viv and John's music continued to fill the pub, a sense of urgency gripped Lin. While the arsonist remained at large and the ghost called for her help, she knew one thing was certain—the stakes were growing higher, and a blaze of worry and uncertainty burned in her brain.

16

The next evening, Lin stood on the stone dust path, her eyes scanning the quiet street for any sign of Libby Hartnett or Viv. The sun had set an hour ago, and the evening air held a slight chill. She shivered and pulled her sweater tighter.

"Lin! We're over here," Viv called, waving from under a big tree. Lin hurried over to join her cousin, relief washing over her as she spotted the familiar figure of their distant relative, Libby Hartnett. Even though she was older, the woman was vibrant, energetic, and hardy.

"Nice to see you." Libby's eyes were steady and calm. "Let's head to William Johnson's grave. Anton researched where it's located so I know where to go." The woman was already moving toward the cemetery gate as they flicked on their flashlights. Lin exchanged a glance with Viv before they followed Libby into the graveyard. The night air grew a little cooler as they walked past the wrought iron fence to the entrance and made their way along the rows of gravestones. The three women walked in silence, the air filled with a symphony from the crickets punctuated by the occasional hoot of an owl. The scent of freshly cut grass wafted past the threesome.

Lin ran her fingers over the top of a tombstone, the cool granite rough under her skin. Viv's hand clasped hers and she squeezed her cousin's hand in return.

"Tell me this is going to be okay. Tell me what we're going to do won't hurt us," Viv requested.

With a smile, Lin said, "We'll be fine, not to worry."

"Here it is," Libby announced, stopping in front of an old worn gravestone bearing the name of William Johnson. Libby reached out to touch the cold stone, her fingers tracing the engraved letters. The woman turned to Lin and Viv. "We have powerful gifts that we must use for good. Since you believe William Johnson is somehow connected to the arsonist, he may have important information to share with us."

"Okay," Lin said, taking a deep breath. "Let's try to find out what William wants."

"Place your hand on the tombstone and concentrate," Libby instructed.

Lin hesitated for a few seconds before doing as she was told, and for a moment, Viv placed her hand on her cousin's shoulder for support.

As they waited, the wind rustled through the trees, and the shadows grew longer under the moonlight. Lin felt a strange sensation pass through her, like a cold finger moving down her spine, and suddenly, she knew they weren't alone.

"William Johnson," Libby called softly. "We are here to help. Please, show us something that will lead us to the arsonist." With a calm and steady voice, she told the cousins, "We need to join our energies and concentrate on the arsonist."

Lin glanced at Viv, who gave her an encouraging nod. The three held hands, forming a tight circle around the gravestone, their fingers entwined.

"Close your eyes," Libby whispered. "Take a deep breath, and imagine a light connecting us."

As Lin followed Libby's instructions, she felt an energy surge through her like an electric current running from her fingertips to her heart. The sensation was both invigorating and unsettling.

"Let the light expand," Libby continued, her voice now barely audible. "Let it reach out to William, to the arsonist, and to the fires that have struck fear into the Nantucket community."

Lin squeezed her eyes shut, focusing on the energy flowing between them. She felt the world around her fade away, as it was replaced by an ethereal landscape where shadows danced and whispers echoed.

"Remember," Libby murmured, "we're looking for answers, not more questions. Let the truth reveal itself."

And then, without warning, the vision came.

A house ablaze, its once-charming exterior reduced to a twisted, blackened shell. Flames licked hungrily at the structure, devouring everything in its path. Smoke billowed into the air, choking out the view of the stars.

The screams were almost unbearable – cries of terror and anguish that pierced Lin's heart. She could feel the heat radiating off the fire, scorching her skin and singeing her hair.

And there, amidst the chaos and destruction, stood a slim figure. Shrouded in darkness, the person moved away from the inferno with quick, agile steps, their face hidden beneath a hood. His hands were gloved, but Lin noticed something glinting in the flickering firelight - a small, lit-up matchbook.

"Who are you?" Lin called out, trying to keep her voice steady despite the fear and confusion coursing through her veins. "Why are you doing this?"

But the figure didn't answer. Instead, he simply melted into the shadows, leaving Lin with nothing but a sense of dread and desperation.

"Enough," Libby said suddenly, breaking the connection between them. Lin's eyes snapped open, and she found herself once again standing in the cemetery, the vision fading like a dying ember.

"Did you see that?" Lin gasped, her heart racing. "The fire... the screams... that person..."

The chilling screams from the vision still echoed in Lin's ears, making her shudder. She felt light-headed and swayed on her feet. Viv grabbed her arm to steady her, her own face ashen and pinched with worry.

"Are you okay?" Viv asked, her voice trembling slightly.

"Y-yeah," Lin stuttered, trying to regain her composure. "That was just ... so intense."

Viv nodded, her face pale and her eyes wide. "I

saw it, too, but who is he? And what does he want from setting the fires?"

"Here." Libby handed them each a bottle of water she had retrieved from her bag. "Drink."

They sank down onto the grass, their backs against the cool stone of a nearby tombstone. The women drank from their bottles; the water soothing their dry throats and helping to clear their minds.

"All right," Lin began, taking a deep breath, "we need to figure out what that vision meant. There must be some clue in there to help us find the arsonist."

"Agreed," Libby said, her blue eyes sharp and focused. "I noticed that the figure was wearing some sort of hood to conceal their face. Did either of you see any other distinguishing features?"

Viv shook her head. "Not really. He was too fast, almost like he knew we were watching him."

Lin frowned, lost in thought. "But why would the ghost of William Johnson lead us to that vision? What can we learn from it? What does he want us to know?"

"Perhaps," Libby mused, "he's trying to alert us to a pattern, something that connects these fires in some way."

"Or maybe there's someone specific that he

wants us to know about," Viv suggested, her eyes widening at the thought. "Maybe someone who's in danger right now."

Determination hardened Lin's features. "We need to stop this arsonist before anyone else gets hurt. If William is trying to help us, we owe it to him to listen."

"Agreed," Viv said with a nod as the women stood up.

A chill wind swept through the cemetery sending goosebumps up Lin's arms and making her shiver. She pulled her sweater tighter as she walked, unable to shake off the eerie feeling that had settled over her since the vision. It was like the very air around them had become charged with energy.

"That was intense. Is everything all right?" Viv asked, concern etched on her face.

Lin nodded, trying to smile reassuringly. "Yeah, just ... I don't know. It feels like there's something more we're supposed to see here."

As they passed by an old, moss-covered gravestone, Lin stopped abruptly. A strange sensation coursed through her like an icy hand sliding over her skin. The hair on her arms stood up, and she found herself instinctively reaching out to steady herself against the headstone.

"Lin?" Libby's voice sounded far away, as if she were speaking from the other end of a long tunnel.

"Wait," Lin whispered, her eyes darting around the graveyard. "Do you feel that?"

"Feel what?" Viv asked in confusion as she glanced around nervously.

"Something," Lin murmured, trying to pinpoint the source of the sensation. "I don't know. It's unlike anything I've ever felt before."

"Is William Johnson's ghost trying to communicate with you again?" Libby asked, her eyes narrowed in thought.

"I don't think that's it," Lin said hesitantly, though she couldn't rid herself of the nagging feeling that there was more to this sensation than met the eye.

As if in answer to her unspoken question, Lin suddenly spotted a figure standing near one of the graves ... a man, his face pale and translucent, dressed in clothing that seemed a century out of date. He looked at her with a kind, almost sorrowful expression, his eyes filled with an unspoken plea for help.

"William," she breathed, her heart racing as she recognized the ghost from their previous encounters. "You're here."

"Lin, what do you see?" Viv asked, her voice hushed and anxious.

"William Johnson's ghost," Lin replied, unable to tear her gaze away from him. "He's right there, standing by that grave."

"Can he hear us?" Libby inquired, her eyes wide with wonder.

"Yes ... I think so," Lin said, her attention still focused on the ghostly figure before her.

"Ask him if he has any more information about the arsonist," Viv urged, her voice trembling with a mixture of fear and excitement.

"William," Lin called out hesitantly, "do you have any clues for us? Any information that could help us find the person responsible for the fires?"

The ghost of William Johnson seemed to consider her question for a moment, his face a mixture of sadness and determination. Then, slowly, he raised a hand and pointed to a spot just beyond the grave where he stood.

"Over there," Lin relayed to Viv and Libby, following his silent direction. "He's pointing at something over there."

"Let's go see," Libby suggested, and the three women made their way toward the indicated area, their hearts pounding with anticipation and uncertainty. As they approached, Lin felt that whatever they found there would be a crucial piece of the puzzle - a vital clue that would bring them one step closer to solving the mystery of the arsonist.

Her eyes scanned the area, searching for anything that might be a clue.

"Is there another ghost?" Viv asked quietly, her voice tense with anticipation.

"I don't see any," Lin replied, her heart racing as she continued to search. She urged herself not to overlook even the smallest detail. Her senses were heightened, attuned to the slightest shift in energy or the faintest whisper of movement, but aside from William Johnson's ghost, the cemetery seemed empty of any other supernatural visitors.

"Maybe it's just William," Libby suggested. "Maybe he's the key to all of this."

"Maybe," Lin agreed, feeling a small knot of disappointment in her stomach.

"Let's keep moving around," Viv said, nodding toward the spot beyond the grave that William had pointed to. "There has to be something there."

As the women walked forward, Lin glanced back at William's ghost, his kind eyes still locked onto hers, silently urging her on. The wind picked up, rustling the leaves in the surrounding trees.

In that instant, like a candle's flame snuffed out by the breeze, William's ghost sparked and vanished. Lin blinked, startled, and stared at the empty space where he had been standing moments ago.

"Did you see that?" she asked, her voice barely a whisper as she turned to Viv and Libby.

"See what?" Viv asked, her eyes wide with concern.

"William," Lin replied, the words catching in her throat. "He ... he just disappeared."

"Maybe that's all he could do for us," Libby said gently, placing a comforting hand on Lin's shoulder. "Maybe he used all of his energy to share that vision."

Lin nodded, feeling a sense of loss at the ghost's sudden departure. She had never met William Johnson in life, yet his spirit had entrusted her with an important mission – and she was determined not to fail.

"Come on," Viv urged, breaking the solemn silence. "Let's keep looking."

Walking around the headstones, they continued moving their flashlights about the grass for another fifteen minutes. With a heavy sigh, Lin looked at Viv and Libby, her eyes still a bit blurry from the vision they'd shared. A thick fog had begun to settle over the cemetery.

"Let's go," Lin said. "We need to figure out our next steps and we're not making any progress here."

They walked slowly, feeling the cool dampness in the air as they made their way through the rows of headstones.

"Where do we start?" Viv asked, her brow furrowed in thought. "Who is this arsonist? And why are they doing this?"

"Those are the questions we need to answer," Lin replied.

Libby squeezed Lin's hand before letting go. "I have a feeling William's ghost brought us together for a reason."

"I think so, too," said Lin, her thoughts racing with possibilities. She felt the familiar tingle of intuition, like a beacon guiding her forward.

The women reached the cemetery gate, pausing for a moment to gather their thoughts.

"Let's start by looking into any connections between the victims," Lin suggested. "Maybe there's a pattern we're not seeing yet."

"Good idea," Viv agreed. "I'll talk to more of my neighbors to find out if they heard or saw anything the night of the fire."

"Meanwhile, I'll contact some of my fellow intuits," Libby offered. "Perhaps one of them can sense something we haven't."

"Sounds like a plan," Lin said, nodding her approval. "Let's meet up at Viv's bookshop tomorrow morning to talk things over."

As the women parted ways, a strange mix of fear and anticipation came over Lin. The road ahead would be filled with uncertainty, but she knew that she was meant to walk it. It was her purpose, her gift - not only to see the ghosts that lingered in the shadows, but to help them find peace and justice.

17

Under the shade of a massive oak tree, Lin and Leonard sat at a wooden picnic table in the park, their work boots still covered in soil from the morning's landscaping. The sun was warm on their faces as they unwrapped sandwiches. Lin poured some water into a bowl and shook some kibble into a second bowl for the dog.

"Did Brian Hunter work with you this morning?" Lin asked, taking a bite of her sandwich.

"He did," Leonard replied, wiping his mouth with a napkin. "Poor kid's been through so much."

Lin nodded and sighed. "It's heartbreaking. How did he do with the landscaping?"

"Remarkable, if I'm honest," Leonard said, a hint of pride in his voice. "That boy worked hard and didn't complain once. You should've seen him digging holes for the shrubs, precise and efficient. He even asked good questions about the design, soil composition, and choice of plants. I think he's got a real knack for it. I was pleased."

"Really? That's great to hear," Lin said, smiling. "Maybe we can find more opportunities for him to work with us. It could be good for him."

"I think he'd like that. I'm impressed with how he handled the tasks I gave him," Leonard added, pausing to take a sip from his thermos.

They continued eating, enjoying the warmth of the sun on their skin and the gentle rustle of leaves above them. Lin thought about Brian, the weight of his loss, and how important it was to find something positive to focus on. She felt grateful for her own life, even for the ghosts that haunted her, and the mystery she was committed to solving.

As Lin took another bite of her sandwich, she glanced at Leonard. "It's such a heartbreaking story, isn't it? Losing both parents when you're only a teen."

"It sure is," Leonard agreed, his voice softening. "And with Paul and Beth doing their best to keep the family together, it's a lot of pressure on them, too. A tough situation."

"Definitely," Lin nodded, her thoughts turning to her own parents' tragic accident. She knew all too well the pain and confusion that came with loss.

The scent of the sea breeze filled the air as they continued their conversation.

Lin decided to share her recent experience at the graveyard with Leonard. "I went to the cemetery with Viv and Libby the other night. We were trying to communicate with the ghost of William Johnson."

"Really?" Leonard asked, raising an eyebrow. "Tell me about it, Coffin." The man took a long sip from his thermos.

"So," Lin said, her voice dropping to a whisper as she recounted the events, "we went there hoping to get some answers about the fires on the island. You know I've been seeing William Johnson's ghost, and we thought maybe he could give us some clues about the arsonist."

"Interesting," Leonard said, his practical nature coming through despite his own experience with the supernatural. "And how did that go?"

Lin sighed, frustration evident on her face. "Not as well as we hoped. Viv, Libby, and I formed a circle around William's grave, hoping that our connection to each other would help us communicate with him," she explained, recalling the eerie atmosphere of the cemetery. "We held hands and tried to open our minds to whatever messages William might have for us."

"Did it work?" Leonard asked, leaning forward, his sandwich momentarily forgotten.

"Not really. We each experienced a similar vision. We saw a house burning down. The heat was intense, and we could hear the crackling of the wood as it burned.

We heard screams."

"Terrifying," Leonard nodded. "I'm glad I missed it."

"It was terrible," Lin admitted, shuddering at the memory, "but there was something else ... there was a slender figure standing near the burning house, wearing a hood and holding a lit matchbook. We couldn't see his face, but the presence felt menacing like they were the one responsible for the fire. I believe that figure is the arsonist. When we came out of the hallucination, William appeared and pointed to something in the cemetery. Viv, Libby, and I searched high and low, but whatever it was that William wanted us to see, it remained hidden. We couldn't find what he was trying to indicate to us." Lin rubbed some dirt from her arm. "It felt like we were missing something," she continued, her voice filled with uncertainty. "The thing is, we don't know who this person is or why they're doing this. And we didn't get any further information from William's ghost."

"Still, it's something," Leonard said, trying to remain optimistic. "You just need to figure out how to use this information to catch the arsonist."

Lin nodded, her determination renewed. "You're right. We can't let this person continue to terrorize our community. If William Johnson can help us, maybe we'll be able to stop them before they strike again."

"Strange, isn't it?" Leonard mused, rubbing his chin thoughtfully. "You'd think a ghost trying to communicate with you would make it a bit easier on you."

"Apparently not. It's never worked that way," Lin told him, frustration lacing her voice. "Libby suggested making our circle next to William's grave. We thought it might help if we were near his body," Lin explained, the memory of their fruitless efforts still fresh in her mind. "We were so hopeful that being near William's grave would give us a stronger connection, but it just left us more confused than ever."

Leonard nodded slowly, taking in the information. "Well, maybe there's something else in the cemetery that you overlooked. It might be worth another visit."

"Maybe." Lin hesitated, her fingers fidgeting with the edge of her napkin. "I just don't know what we're missing. We tried so hard to understand what he wanted us to see, but it was like grasping at smoke."

"Sometimes these things take time, Coffin," Leonard reassured her, placing a comforting hand on her shoulder. "You'll figure it out. You always do."

"Thanks." Lin smiled weakly. "I just hope we can solve this mystery before it's too late."

"Knowing you, I'm sure you were thorough," Leonard said, "but sometimes, things just slip through the cracks. You might find something new if you take a fresh look at the situation."

Nicky woofed in agreement.

Lin sighed and took a sip from her water bottle, enjoying the cool liquid against her parched throat. "You're right. Maybe I was so focused on the ghost and what he was trying to tell us that I didn't pay enough attention to our surroundings."

"Exactly," Leonard agreed, wiping his hands on a napkin. "And you know how these old cemeteries can be – full of hidden nooks and crannies."

"Okay." Lin steadied herself, determination

surging through her veins. "I'll go back to the cemetery tonight."

Leonard nodded approvingly. "I can go with you."

Lin smiled. "Maybe we'll find something that leads us right to the arsonist."

"Miracles do happen," Leonard teased.

Lin leaned forward against the picnic table, closing her eyes for a few seconds and soaking in the warmth of the sun. She took a deep breath. The tranquility of the park offered a brief moment of peace from their earlier conversation about the cemetery and the arsonist.

"I've always admired your ability to see ghosts," Leonard told her. "It's something I never completely understood, even when I could see my wife's ghost before she crossed over."

"I don't understand it either," Lin replied, opening her eyes to meet his gaze, "but it's just always been a part of me."

"It makes you ... interesting."

Lin laughed. "That's one way to put it."

"When we finish work today, we'll head to the cemetery, and we won't leave until we find whatever it is that William's ghost wants us to see."

"We might be there all night," Lin said with a

grin, "but we'll approach the search with a positive attitude. Last time, we overlooked something. This time we'll find it."

Leonard nodded. "I like the sound of that."

"Good," Lin replied, "because tonight, we'll need all the help we can get."

18

The sun dipped low on the horizon, casting a warm orange glow over the cemetery as Lin, Leonard, and Nicky walked along the narrow dirt path. The air was thick with humidity; sweat beaded on Lin's forehead as she wiped it away with the back of her hand. She could feel the tension in her shoulders, so she took a deep breath and tried to relax her muscles.

"William Johnson's grave should be right around here," Lin said, scanning the rows of tombstones. "It was dark when I was here before and I wasn't paying close attention."

"Why not, Coffin? Afraid of ghosts?" Leonard kidded.

Lin just shook her head at the man's joke.

"Maybe the cur will find something." Leonard watched Nicky trot around and sniff at the ground, his tail wagging as he explored his surroundings.

"He's good at flushing things out." Lin stopped. "Here it is. Here's William Johnson's grave."

Leonard let out a sigh. "A terrible way to die. He was probably trying to save his family that night. A sad, sad story."

"William was standing behind the grave the other night. He pointed in that direction." Lin raised her hand and gestured.

Leonard said, "Okay. Let's keep our eyes open. We might be looking for something out of the ordinary."

They began to walk around, glancing here and there as they moved around the space.

"Could William have been pointing to something in the distance?" Leonard looked beyond the confines of the cemetery. "Maybe what he was trying to show you isn't in here."

Lin turned to her friend, considering his suggestion and trying to recall William's gesture from the other night. "I don't think so. William pointed closer to the ground, not off in the distance. I'm pretty sure what he wants us to find is here in the cemetery."

They continued to walk around the graves looking for whatever might be a clue to the house fires.

After nearly forty-five minutes had passed, Lin sighed and pushed a strand of damp hair from her face. "I just wish we had something more solid to go on. It's like trying to find a needle in a haystack."

Leonard placed a reassuring hand on her shoulder, his warm smile cutting through the gloom. "Don't give up yet, Coffin. You'll find it when you least expect it."

She nodded, touched by his faith in her abilities. As they continued their search, they moved back in the direction of William Johnson's grave, and still unable to find something, a growing sense of frustration began to build in Lin.

What were they even looking for? A ghostly clue hidden among the graves, or some solid proof that would lead them to the arsonist?

"Ugh, this is useless," Lin exclaimed, kicking at a pebble. "There's nothing here ... no sign, no message, no helpful ghost, nothing."

"Patience, Coffin," Leonard chided gently. "Even the smallest detail could prove to be useful. Remember, we have the advantage of knowing there's a link between the past and present fires. We just need to find what connects them."

"You're right," she conceded. "Let's keep looking. Maybe we'll find something we missed." Lin took a deep breath, forcing herself to calm down. Leonard was right; getting angry wouldn't solve anything. She needed to focus. Scanning the area once more, she hoped for a breakthrough.

"It's here somewhere. We just have to see it. Your ghost wouldn't send you on a wild goose chase," Leonard told her, his voice steady and supportive. Together, they continued their search, Nicky bounding along beside them.

After another half hour of picking around the grass, Nicky's ears perked up, and he began sniffing the ground with interest. Lin watched as her dog darted between graves, his tail wagging excitedly. She followed him, Leonard at her side, until they found themselves standing before an old, worn headstone partially obscured by long grass.

"Look at this," Lin said softly, crouching down to read the inscription. "It's Nathan Post's grave. He's the boy Arthur Radcliffe ordered to set fire to William's house. He was just a teen when he died."

Leonard brushed a fern out of the way as he

peered closer at Nathan's worn headstone. "Fifteen years old," he murmured, a hint of sadness in his voice. "Such a short life."

"Hey, do you notice something odd?" Lin asked, her forehead wrinkling as she looked around. "There isn't anything about his family on the headstone. Often, it says 'son of so-and-so. It's only his name, birth year, and death year.'"

"True," Leonard agreed, looking at the surrounding graves. "I don't see any other graves with the name Post nearby."

"I wonder why not." When Lin stood up and brushed off her knees, the air around her seemed to thicken, and she felt a sudden wave of dizziness wash over her. She reached out, grasping Leonard's arm for support.

"You okay, Coffin?"

"I just got light-headed for a second. It must be the humidity." After taking a long swallow from her water bottle, she searched around for any members of the Post family. "Why isn't Nathan buried close to his family members? And why is he near William Johnson's grave?"

"Curious." Leonard echoed Lin's thoughts as he placed a hand on his chin, deep in thought.

Lin paced around the small plot, her frustration from earlier now replaced by questions. The sun had dipped below the horizon and the air buzzed with the distant hum of cicadas, their chorus filling the humid evening. Sweat trickled down Lin's back, but she barely noticed, her mind racing with questions.

As they were about to walk away from Nathan's grave, an unusual sensation flooded Lin's veins.

"Leonard," she said, her voice strained. "Nathan Post set fire to William's house in 1901. William must have wanted me to see the boy's grave."

"Remember, Arthur Radcliffe paid the teen to set that fire," Leonard reminded her gently, his concern evident in his voice. "It wasn't solely the boy's decision. The teen was poor and his family was suffering. He was desperate."

"Right," Lin agreed as she took a deep breath, inhaling the scent of damp earth and fragrant flowers that surrounded them. "There has to be a reason why this boy is buried so close to William and why his family isn't mentioned on his headstone. This teenager was responsible for setting the fire at William's house, so isn't it odd that the two would be buried so close together?"

Leonard's brow furrowed. "It's definitely peculiar."

"Exactly." Lin bit her lip, feeling the weight of the mystery bearing down on her. "I need to talk to Anton." Her eyes widened as the implications dawned on her. "Wait a minute. Arthur Radcliffe paid the poor boy to set fire to William's house. Is someone paying the current-day arsonist?"

Leonard considered Lin's words. "Maybe," he finally answered, his voice holding a note of caution, "or maybe there's another reason we can't see yet. Is someone intimidating or threatening the arsonist to set the fires?"

A creeping sense of unease settled around Lin like a cold fog. She could almost feel the restless energy of her ghost, reaching out to her for help.

Lin looked down at Nathan Post's grave, the fading letters etched into the weathered stone telling the story of a life cut short, and she felt a strong connection to the young boy from so long ago.

"This is the clue William wanted me to find," Lin whispered. "Finding Nathan Post's grave is a clue to what's going on with the recent fires. We just have to figure out what it means."

"You'll find the answers. Stay focused," Leonard urged her gently, his strong hand on her arm providing a welcome anchor to the present. "You'll find what you need. Just give it time."

As Lin, Leonard, and Nicky walked through the graveyard back to the truck, she couldn't escape the heavy presence of her ghost. It was as if he were calling out to her, pleading for her help.

"Time is something we might not have," Lin said softly, feeling the cold chill of fear run over her skin.

19

Lin and Jeff bustled around, setting up for their potluck cookout. The couple had invited Viv, John, Leonard and Heather, and Paul, Beth, and Brian.

"Everything looks perfect," Jeff said, wrapping his arm around his wife's waist and planting a kiss on her cheek.

"Thanks, we did a good job. I just hope everyone has a nice time," Lin replied, looking over the table laden with food and drinks, ensuring that nothing was amiss.

"Lin, Jeff!" Viv called out, waving enthusiastically as she and John approached around the corner of the house. "This is such a great idea. I brought desserts, an apple pie and an ice cream cake."

"Yum." Lin embraced her cousin warmly and then hugged John. "We're so glad you could make it."

Leonard and Heather showed up next with Leonard carrying a bowl of green salad and Heather bringing a potato salad.

"These look delicious," Lin told them as Jeff took the bowls and set them down on the serving table.

"The deck and patio look so nice." Heather admired the landscaping of greenery and flowers.

Paul, Beth, and Brian Hunter arrived a few minutes later. Beth carried a pasta salad and Paul had three six packs of beer.

Brian told Lin, "We brought the stuff to make s'mores later."

"Thanks," Lin said giving the teen a hug. "That will be fun."

"I brought some craft beer," Paul chimed in, setting the six packs on the table. "I hope you like it."

John looked at the beer. "Nantucket Seas? I've never seen this brand before."

"Is this something new?" Viv asked. "I'm not familiar with it."

"The famous Nantucket Seas beer." Leonard smiled. "I've heard great things about it, Paul."

"Thanks, Leonard," Paul replied, a note of pride

in his voice. "I've worked hard on perfecting the recipe. I'm really happy with how it came out."

"What a second," Jeff said. "You made this?"

"I did. A friend and I have been working on crafting our own brand of beer for a few years. We have two we're especially pleased with. We approached a couple of specialty shops and a pub in town and they agreed to carry it. We're excited. It's a small thing, but it's a start."

"Oh, my gosh." Lin hugged the young man. "Congratulations."

"And it's not a small thing," Jeff told him. "Getting your first customers is a huge thing."

"So much goes into a business before the first sales come in," John agreed. "Getting stores to carry it is a very big step."

"We had some pens, coasters, and matchbooks printed up with the name of our beer and the name of the pub and shops who are carrying them so they could hand them out to customers."

"Smart marketing," Viv told him.

"Can I open one?" Lin asked.

"Of course." Paul beamed.

Lin used the opener to pop the cap off and poured the golden liquid into a glass before sipping. Her eyes widened. "This is amazing. It's so good."

More bottles were opened so the others could taste Paul's creation.

"I love it. Let's all toast to Paul's success," Heather suggested, raising a bottle of the amber liquid in her hand.

"Here's to Nantucket Seas!" they all chorused, clinking bottles and glasses together before taking more swallows.

Viv said, "I can see this beer becoming a big hit."

"Thanks, everyone," Paul said, his cheeks coloring slightly at the praise. "It's been a labor of love."

"Keep up the good work," Jeff added, patting Paul on the shoulder. "We're all rooting for you."

As the conversation continued with everyone offering their support and encouragement to Paul, Lin stole a few glances at Brian. The teen seemed fine, laughing and chatting with the others, but Lin could sense the angst beneath the surface.

"Brian's really going through a tough time," she whispered to Jeff, as they stood at the edge of the deck. "I just wish there was some way we could help him."

"Maybe talking to him about your own experiences would be a good place to start," Jeff suggested gently. "You've been through a lot, and you've come out strong on the other side. That might give him some hope."

Lin nodded thoughtfully, her eyes never leaving Brian. She knew that words alone wouldn't heal the pain he was feeling, but if she could offer even a small measure of comfort, it would be worth it.

The late afternoon sun shone across the small yard as Lin watched her friends and family laughing and talking, the sound of metal clinking against metal punctuating the air. The friendly competition of horseshoes had begun, and she couldn't help but smile as she saw the joy on everyone's faces.

"Nice throw, John!" Leonard called out, clapping his hands in support as Viv's husband scored another point.

"Thanks," John replied, grinning from ear to ear. "I'm only just warming up," he kidded.

"We'll see about that," Leonard shot back with a laugh, stepping up to take his turn. With a smooth motion, he sent the horseshoe sailing through the air, narrowly missing the stake but eliciting cheers from the group nonetheless.

As the game continued, Lin stood back for a moment, taking it all in. She could feel the warmth of the sun on her face and the gentle breeze rustling her hair. She loved moments like this – when everything seemed right with the world.

"Lin! You're up!" Heather called, beckoning her to join the fun.

"All right, all right." Lin laughed, stepping up to the makeshift line drawn in the dirt. Gripping the cold iron horseshoe, she took a deep breath, focused her aim, and tossed it toward the stake. To her surprise, it landed just inches away, earning her a round of applause from the others.

"Nice one," Viv exclaimed, clapping her hands enthusiastically. "You've got quite an arm there."

"Thanks, cousin," Lin replied, feeling a surge of happiness at her unexpected success. "Beginner's luck, I guess?"

"Or natural talent," Jeff chimed in.

Before long, the smell of sizzling burgers, veggie burgers, corn, and grilled vegetables wafted through the air, signaling that it was almost time to eat. The group gathered around the table, their mouths watering in anticipation as they filled their plates with heaping servings of food.

"Everything looks delicious," Heather remarked, admiring the colorful array of dishes before her.

"It sure does," Leonard added, taking a bite of his

burger. "Lin, Jeff, you've outdone yourselves. This burger is great."

"Thanks," Lin replied, beaming at the compliments. "We couldn't have done it without everyone's contributions."

"True," Viv chimed in, popping a cherry tomato into her mouth. "These salads are amazing, and Beth, your pasta dish is to die for."

"It's my mom's recipe," Beth replied softly, a hint of sadness in her eyes as she remembered her late mother.

Lin caught the subtle shift in mood and quickly tried to lighten the atmosphere. "Well, I think we can all agree that this has been a fantastic meal. And speaking of amazing dishes, Paul, those craft beers of yours really hit the spot."

Paul raised his bottle in appreciation. "I'm glad everyone enjoyed them."

As the meal continued, Lin found herself drawn back into the sounds of the gathering – the laughter, the clinking of silverware, and the satisfied sighs of friends and family enjoying good food and company. But even amidst the happiness, she couldn't help but keep one eye on Brian, Paul, and Beth hoping that the warmth and love surrounding them would be a small measure of comfort.

As the sun dipped below the horizon, Brian stood up from his chair. "I think I'll take a walk down to the pond," he announced, looking as though he needed some time alone.

"Mind if the cat and dog join you?" Lin asked.

"Sure," he replied with a half-smile. "Come on, Nicky and Queenie." The two animals eagerly bounded after him as he disappeared into the woods behind Lin's house.

"All right, everyone," Jeff called out, clapping his hands together. "Let's get this fire pit going." He began stacking logs in the center of the stone circle, arranging them to ensure a good blaze.

The others moved their chairs closer to the fire pit, anticipating the warmth and camaraderie that would come once the flames were lit. Viv wrapped herself in a soft shawl, while Leonard helped Heather adjust her seat.

Lin watched them all settle in, but her thoughts remained on Brian. She wished she could do more to help him. She understood how much harder things could be for a young teen.

"Here we go," Jeff exclaimed as he struck a match, igniting the kindling beneath the logs. The fire roared to life, crackling and snapping as the flames leapt higher. Everyone instinctively leaned toward the comforting heat, their faces illuminated by the flickering light.

"Ah, there's nothing like a fire on a cool evening," Leonard remarked, stretching out his legs and crossing his ankles. "It's the perfect way to end a day like this."

"Absolutely," Heather agreed, nestling closer to him. "And we have the perfect company to share it with."

"Cheers to that," John added, raising his bottle of Nantucket Seas in a toast.

"Cheers," everyone echoed, clinking their bottles and glasses together.

As the fire continued to burn, the conversation flowed easily among the group. They discussed everything from the latest news on the island to childhood memories and shared experiences. Laughter rang out, punctuated by the occasional distant bark from the dog as he chased after the cat through the woods at the back of the property.

But amidst the fun atmosphere, Lin was concerned for Brian. She knew that grief had a way of isolating people, even in the midst of friends and family, and she wondered if, beneath his strong facade, Brian was feeling lost in this new, parentless world.

"Excuse me for a moment," Lin whispered to Jeff, her eyes straying toward the dark woods where Brian had disappeared with the animals. "I need to check on something."

"Sure," he replied, giving her hand a reassuring squeeze. "Take your time."

With a quick glance at the circle of friends around the fire, Lin quietly slipped away, following the path that Brian had taken. The firelight gradually faded behind her, leaving her to navigate by the silvery glow of the moon filtering through the trees.

Back at the fire pit, Viv and John shared playful banter while Heather and Leonard discussed an upcoming charity event. The warm glow of the fire flickered against their faces, casting shadows that danced and jumped.

"Brian?" Lin called, listening intently for any sign of him.

"Over here."

She followed the sound to find Brian sitting on a fallen log near the edge of the pond, his head hanging low as he clutched a half-empty beer bottle. The cat and dog lay nearby, watching him with worry in their eyes. Lin hesitated for a moment, taking in the scene before her. She knew that Brian was struggling, but she also recognized the dangers of underage drinking.

"Mind if I join you?" Lin asked, taking a seat beside him.

"Sure," Brian replied, his voice heavy.

"Hey," she said softly, approaching the situation with concern. "I'm not here to judge you, but you know that's not the answer, right?"

Brian looked up at her, his eyes glassy and red-rimmed. He didn't say anything, but the weight of his silence spoke volumes.

"Believe me, I understand the pain you're going through," Lin continued, her voice gentle yet firm, "but numbing yourself with alcohol won't make it go away. It'll only make things harder in the long run."

The wind whispered through the trees, carrying with it the faint echoes of laughter from the fire pit. For a moment, Lin wondered if she was making any headway with Brian, or if her words were simply getting lost in the darkness around them.

"Look," she said, her tone softening. "I know you're hurting, and I wish I could take that pain away for you, but the best thing you can do right now is to surround yourself with people who care about you, people like your brother and sister, friends, and us."

Brian stared at the beer bottle in his hand, the amber liquid reflecting the moonlight like a distorted mirror. With a resigned sigh, he set it down on the ground.

"Maybe you're right," he whispered, his voice barely audible.

Lin hesitated for a moment before deciding to share her own experience with Brian. "In some ways, I know what you're going through," she began, her voice empathetic and sincere. "I lost my parents when I was young. I was only a little kid at the time and didn't understand what had happened."

Brian glanced at her, surprise flickering across his features before he looked down at his feet. "You did?" he mumbled, kicking a small rock on the ground.

"Yeah. Being little when they died, I didn't understand any of it. One day, they were there, and the next, they weren't, but when I was around your age, it all hit me and I grieved for my parents for a long time. I understand how hard it can be."

Brian nodded.

Lin went on, "It was really tough, but I learned some things that helped me cope, and maybe they'll help you, too." She paused, taking a deep breath as memories of her own losses came flooding back.

"One of the most important things is to let yourself grieve. It's okay to be sad, angry, or even numb. Just don't bottle everything up inside."

Brian's shoulders slumped slightly as if a heavy weight had settled upon them. "I just ... I don't know what to do anymore, Lin," he confessed, his voice cracking. "It's like I'm drifting in this huge sea, and there's no one there to anchor me."

Lin reached out and gently squeezed his arm, offering him a comforting smile. "That's a completely normal feeling, and while I can't bring your parents back, I want you to know that you're not alone. You have people who care about you and will be here for you, Paul and Beth, Jeff and me, Viv and John, Leonard and Heather."

"Really?" Brian asked, his eyes searching hers for reassurance.

"Absolutely," Lin confirmed, her determination evident in her gaze. "And another thing that might help is finding something to focus on, a purpose or a goal. It could be anything – school, work, hobbies. Just something that gives you a reason to keep moving forward."

"Is that what helped you?

Lin considered his question, her eyes distant as she recalled those years with her grandfather. "Yes, but what also helped me was allowing myself time to grieve, to feel the pain of losing my parents, and accepting that it was okay to miss them." She took a slow, steadying breath. "I found ways to keep their memory alive, like talking about them with my grandfather or visiting their graves. It didn't take the pain away, but it made it more bearable."

Brian's forehead scrunched up as he considered her words. "Thanks, Lin," he said quietly, offering her a small, tentative smile. "I just ... I miss them so much."

"Of course you do," Lin acknowledged, her heart aching for the pain he was enduring. "And you always will, but time does help. It won't make the loss go away, but it will become more bearable. You'll never forget your parents, and you shouldn't, but you'll learn to live without them, just like I did."

Brian seemed to absorb her words, his body trembling ever so slightly. A single tear escaped from his eye, trailing down his cheek before he hastily wiped it away.

"Hey," Lin said softly, reaching out to touch his arm. "It's okay to cry. It's okay to let it out. Tears are a good thing."

The dam broke. Brian's shoulders shook as he sobbed, his face crumpling with a raw, aching grief.

Lin pulled him into a tight embrace, her heart breaking for the young man who had lost so much.

"Time will pass," she whispered into his hair as he clung to her. "And with it, the pain will slowly ease. It will be okay. You'll be okay. Just let time pass."

As they stood there, the sounds of laughter and conversation from the fire pit moved through the night. Lin knew that even though the journey ahead would be long and difficult, Brian would have people who could guide him through his troubles – just as her grandfather had done for her.

When the teen's sobs stopped, Lin said, "How about we go make those s'mores?"

Brian wiped at his face and nodded, and they, along with the dog and cat, headed back on the path to the house. When they reached the edge of the woods, the laughter and chatter from their family and friends around the fire pit drifted towards them like a warm embrace.

Lin knew that the road ahead would be difficult for Brian, but she also knew that with the help of loved ones and friends, he and his siblings would find a way to navigate the darkness.

As they rejoined the group by the fire pit, she hoped that Brian would find comfort and strength in the knowledge that he wasn't alone in the waters of loss.

"Hey, you two," Jeff called to them. "What about some of those s'mores?"

"Coming right up," Brian assured him and went to the side table to get the tray of ingredients.

"Everything okay?" Jeff whispered to Lin.

"I think it will be." She gave her husband's hand a squeeze and then walked over to help Brian put together the s'mores.

20

Tapping on his laptop, Anton Wilson pulled up the yellowed letter from 1901 from a historical internet database, his black-framed eyeglasses slipping down his nose as he read the words inked on the fragile paper. Lin leaned closer, her curiosity piqued. She imagined the musty scent of the old document filling the air of Anton's study.

"Listen to this, Lin," Anton said, his voice trembling with excitement. "It's a letter from Arthur Radcliffe to his sister, and it sheds light on young Nathan Post's involvement in the fire."

"Will you read it to me?" Lin urged, her eyes wide with anticipation.

"Yes," Anton agreed, clearing his throat. He began to read aloud:

"Dearest Sister,

I fear I have done a terrible thing. I had no choice but to force young Nathan Post, a mere lad of fourteen, to set the fire that has caused so much devastation. The boy was quite reluctant, pleading with me to spare him the dreadful task, but I could not relent. My own future was at stake, and I threatened to harm his family and report him to the police if he did not comply with my order. Nathan's mother is alone. The family is quite poor. Nathan does all he can to help get food for his mother and sister. The boy was an easy choice for me. I knew I could get him to set fire to William Johnson's house if I used his family as a sort of bait."

Lin's heart ached for Nathan Post ... forced into committing such a horrific act. She couldn't help but wonder what would drive Radcliffe to threaten a child the way he did.

Anton continued reading:

"Please forgive me, dear sister, for I know this is an unforgivable sin. I have destroyed lives and property for my own gain, and I forced an innocent boy to bear the burden of my crimes. I hope one day

Nathan can find it in his heart to forgive me, though I doubt I shall ever be able to forgive myself."

As Anton finished reading the letter, he looked at Lin with sorrowful eyes. "Poor Nathan," he said. "He never had a chance." With a sigh, the historian added, "The police uncovered Radcliffe's part in the arson and murder of the Johnson family. Arthur Radcliffe was found guilty and sent to prison."

Lin felt a rush of anger at the injustice of using a young teen to commit a crime. To think that a young boy had been pushed into such a terrible act and then left to suffer the consequences was almost too much to consider.

Anton said, his eyes distant as he recalled the events of that tragic night, "The fire began in the stables which were attached to the main house and where Nathan had placed the burning lantern. Mr. Johnson, his wife, and their children were trapped inside the house." Anton explained, his voice cracking slightly with emotion, "The fire spread rapidly, fueled by dry wood and strong winds. By the time the townsfolk arrived to help, it was too late. The house had been reduced to ashes, and all within it perished."

"Such a terrible, unnecessary loss," Lin whispered.

"Indeed," Anton agreed, his own eyes glistening. "Nathan was arrested soon after, charged with arson and murder. He died in prison a year later, succumbing to an illness brought on by a virus that spread throughout the facility."

Lin said bitterly, "Poor Nathan paid a heavy price for becoming entangled with Radcliffe's plot."

"True." Anton nodded. "But I have discovered one small act of kindness in this dark tale. William Johnson's brother, Thomas, knowing that Nathan had been coerced into setting the fire, pitied the boy."

"Really?" Lin asked, curious.

"Yes," Anton continued. "After Nathan's death, Thomas Johnson arranged for him to be buried on the edge of the Johnson family plot, close enough to acknowledge his connection to their tragedy, yet separate enough to respect the bounds of propriety. It was a gesture of forgiveness and generosity that I believe still holds meaning today."

"I hope Nathan's spirit was able to find peace," Lin said softly, touched by Thomas' act of compassion.

"Perhaps," Anton agreed, his eyes reflecting the light on the table. "We can hope."

With a heavy heart, Lin stepped out of Anton's house and into the cool evening air. The weight of

Nathan's story pressed down on her, swirling with unanswered questions and the restless energy that always followed her interactions with the dead. She needed to move, to think, to somehow process all she had learned.

She made her way along the quiet streets of Nantucket, her footsteps echoing off the sidewalk. The scent of distant woodsmoke hung in the air. As Lin walked, she felt the shadows of the past stretching out across the town with memories of love, loss, and betrayal.

Passing by "Smitty's Place," the words from the matchbook she'd found days ago played on a loop in her mind, taunting her with their possible significance. Could it be a clue to the arsonist's identity? If so, what connection did Smitty's Place have to the fires? And why would the arsonist leave such an obvious clue behind?

"Think, think," she told herself. "There must be something we're missing."

As she wandered further into town, she noticed lamplight spilling out onto the street from Viv's Victus, the popular bookstore-café owned by her cousin. A sudden longing for the comfort of Viv's familiar face washed over her, and she paused, considering whether to go in, but then she decided to just do her errand and head home. With a sigh, she turned away from the inviting warmth of the café and continued on her way.

Her thoughts drifted to the recent fire victims. Did any of them see something more, something they may have passed off as insignificant? Had any of them frequented Smitty's Place?

The pub remained at the front of her thoughts as she walked, and with every step, Lin felt herself growing more resolved to unearth the truth behind the fires for all the victims whose lives had been changed by the arsonist's hand.

"Whoever you are," she whispered into the night, "I will find you, and when I do, justice will finally be served."

She headed to "Sweet Nantucket," a specialty food shop known for its locally sourced food and treats.

"Hi, Lin," greeted the cashier, a young woman with freckles and red curls framing her face.

"Hey, Sarah," Lin replied, trying to muster a smile despite her heavy thoughts. She idly wandered around the small shop; the scent of fresh baked goods and the savory aroma of smoked meats could be smelled on the air. As she chose a few items and approached the register, her gaze fell on a bowl filled with matchbooks, each one adorned with the shop's name and logo. A sudden realization washed over her – if local businesses had their own branded matchbooks, perhaps there was a connection between Smitty's Place and the arsonist.

"Sarah, do you mind if I take one of these?" Lin asked, her voice tense.

"Of course, go ahead," Sarah said.

"Thanks," Lin told the young woman, her fingers trembling as she picked up a matchbook. There, printed in bold letters beneath the shop's familiar logo, was the name of a craft beer: "Nantucket Seas."

Lin's breath caught in her throat. "Isn't that Paul Hunter's beer company?"

"Uh, yeah," Sarah confirmed. "You know Paul. Is everything okay, Lin?"

"Y-yeah... I just remembered something," Lin stammered, forcing a weak smile to mask the jolt of shock and suspicion coursing through her veins. She pocketed the matchbook and turned to leave the store, her mind racing.

"Thanks again, Sarah," she called over her shoulder. "I'll see you later."

As Lin stepped back into the night, her thoughts churned with dark possibilities. Could Paul really be involved in the fires? She had known him for years, but now, with this new piece of evidence, doubt crept into her heart.

Could he really do this? she wondered as she exhaled. *And why would he do it?*

Her hands trembled as she pulled the matchbook from her pocket, running her fingers over the printed words once more. Lin reached for her phone, and her fingers tapped quickly on the screen scrolling through her photos until she found the one she was searching for – an image she had captured at one of the burned-out houses. A matchbook, half-charred and forgotten amongst the debris, had caught her attention back then, though its significance hadn't been immediately apparent.

"Let's see..." Lin whispered, squinting at the picture and zooming in on the partially burnt letters at the bottom of the matchbook. Her heart skipped a beat as she deciphered the familiar words: "ucket Seas."

Dread knotted inside her chest like a heavy stone. The matchbooks from the specialty food store and this charred remnant both bore the name of Paul's craft beer company, Nantucket Seas.

A shiver ran down her spine as she struggled to reconcile the man she knew – a friend and a fellow business owner – with the possibility that he could be the arsonist wreaking havoc on their small community.

Is it really him? she questioned herself, doubt and fear twisting together. *Or is this just a coincidence?*

"Hey, Lin!" came a cheerful voice from behind her, causing her to jump. Jeff appeared, jogging up to her. "What's going on? You look like you've seen a ghost. What's wrong?"

Lin hesitated, swallowing hard. "I ... I may have found a lead on the arsonist."

"Really?" Jeff's eyes widened with surprise and curiosity. "What is it?"

Lin sighed deeply. "Remember the matchbook I found at one of the burned-out houses? I took a picture of it, and the partially burnt letters spelled out 'U-C-K-E-T Seas.' And then today, I saw a matchbook at the specialty food store, and it had 'Nantucket Seas' printed on it – Paul's beer company."

"Paul might really be involved?" Jeff's face paled, his disbelief evident in his expression.

"I don't want to believe it either." Lin's heart ached at the thought of her friend being capable of such destruction. "But we can't ignore the evidence staring us in the face."

Jeff nodded. "It's so hard to believe. If Paul is the

arsonist, what will happen to Brian? Beth would have to become his guardian, I guess. What a mess."

The moon cast a silvery light over the streets as Lin and Jeff walked home. Lin's heart pounded, each beat echoing her growing fear and uncertainty. She knew that digging deeper could unearth answers best left buried, but she couldn't turn away.

Jeff took her hand.

"I don't know what I'd do without you," Lin told him.

Her heart was heavy with worry and disbelief. As she and Jeff walked side by side, she realized that the truth could be as elusive as the ghosts that haunted her.

21

Lin and Jeff's cozy living room was lit up from the evening light pouring through the windows that looked out onto the deck. Viv and John, along with their cat Queenie, had gathered at the house for dinner and movie night, ready to unwind after a long week.

"Here's the famous spinach dip you've been asking for," Lin said, placing the steaming dish on the coffee table, accompanied by an assortment of crackers and breads.

"Finally," Viv exclaimed, scooping up a generous helping with a piece of crusty baguette. "I swear, Lin, I'd marry you for this dip alone if Jeff weren't already in the picture."

Laughter filled the room as John chimed in, "No

pressure, Jeff, but you better watch out. One day she might just steal her away."

"Over my dead body," Jeff replied playfully, wrapping his arm around Lin's shoulders. They shared a quick, loving glance before turning their attention back to their guests.

As they settled into their comfortable seats, the conversation flowed easily among the close-knit group. They discussed the latest island news, including the upcoming charity event organized by Heather Jenness, Leonard's girlfriend. Their banter continued, touching on new movies they wanted to see and possible weekend plans on John and Viv's boat.

"Have you guys heard about that new thriller coming out next week?" John asked, taking a swig of his craft beer. "It's supposed to be a real nail-biter."

"Ooh, sounds interesting. I'd like to see it," Lin said. "Maybe we can all catch it together, make a double date out of it?"

"Count us in," Viv added, exchanging an excited look with John.

As the evening progressed, their laughter mingled with the delicious aromas wafting from the kitchen – roasted garlic and rosemary chicken, buttery mashed potatoes, green beans, salad, and a rich chocolate cake for dessert. When it was ready, they carried platters and dishes out to the deck where the long wooden table was already set with blue plates, silverware, white napkins, glasses, a pitcher of water, and some candles. The strings of tiny white lights Jeff had put up early in May were already shining. The four of them took seats at the table and dug into the food.

"This chicken is delicious," Viv complimented between mouthfuls. "You seriously need to teach me your secret."

"Thanks, Viv," Lin replied with a warm smile.

The weather, the food, and the company were making it a pleasant night together. The laughter, the affection, and the shared experiences Lin and Jeff shared with Viv and John made their time together feel special.

When they were back in the kitchen cleaning up and loading the dishwasher, Lin asked, "Hey, you guys want to see the progress we've made upstairs? We're ready to show you." Her eyes lit up with excitement as she wiped her hands on a dish towel. She and Jeff hadn't shown anyone the second-floor renovations for quite a while, waiting until they'd made a dent in the work.

"We'd love to," Viv exclaimed, setting down her

wine glass. "We're dying to see how everything is coming along."

"Lead the way," John chimed in, grinning.

Lin and Jeff exchanged smiles before leading them up the staircase to the second floor of their antique house that Lin had inherited from her grandfather.

The main floor of the home was designed in a unique "U" shape with one wing housing the primary bedroom and a bathroom and the living room located in the center. There was a second bedroom that Lin used as an office off the living space. The other leg of the "U" housed the kitchen, dining area, and another bathroom. The living room and kitchen had big windows and doors that led out to the large deck.

When the foursome had climbed the staircase, the scent of fresh paint and sawdust lingered in the air, evidence of the countless hours they'd spent working on their home.

"Here's the sitting room," Lin announced as she and the others stepped into the cozy space filled with natural light streaming through the new windows. The soft cream shade on the newly painted walls contrasted beautifully with the dark wooden beams that crisscrossed the ceiling. A plush sofa and a pair of matching armchairs created an inviting seating area, while a bookcase filled with novels and family photos lined one wall.

"Wow, this is gorgeous. I love it," Viv breathed, her eyes wide with admiration as she took in the tasteful decor and attention to detail.

"Isn't it amazing what some elbow grease and determination can do?" Jeff smiled. "It's taken us much longer than expected, but most evenings after work, we've been chipping away at the project."

"Your hard work has definitely paid off," John agreed, admiring how they'd decorated the space. "This room feels so welcoming and comfortable."

"Thanks, John," Lin replied, beaming with satisfaction. She knew they still had a long way to go, but seeing the reaction to the completed sitting room made all those late nights and sore muscles worth it.

"Let me show you the bathroom," Jeff said, guiding them to another door. "It's not quite finished yet, but we're almost there."

As they stepped inside, Lin felt a swell of happiness at how far they'd come. The once-dingy space now boasted a beautiful clawfoot tub, an elegant pedestal sink, and a gleaming row of subway tiles.

"This is really lovely," Viv told them. "I can't believe you two did all this work yourselves. I know

Jeff's renovation and construction skills are top-notch, but tackling all this work after long days at your jobs is really too much."

"Sometimes we feel like it is too much." Lin chuckled.

"But teamwork makes the dream work," Jeff replied with a grin, placing his arm around Lin's shoulders. "We've always been good at working together."

They led Viv and John around the rest of the second floor showing them that the walls had been framed for an office, three additional bedrooms, and another bathroom.

John said, "It's inspiring to see what you two have accomplished, and it makes me want to tackle some projects in our own house."

"Uh oh." Viv laughed.

Jeff suggested, "How about we head back downstairs and break out that chocolate cake? I think it's time for coffee, tea, and dessert."

"Let's go," Viv agreed, already heading to the stairs.

"All right," Lin announced, slicing into the decadent chocolate cake, "take these to the living room. I'm going to go call Nicky and Queenie in. They've been out in the field long enough."

"Good idea," Viv agreed, her eyes lighting up at the sight of the dessert.

As Lin stepped out onto the deck, she was enveloped by the cool evening air. The sun had almost dipped below the horizon and the first stars began to twinkle. She drew in a deep breath, inhaling the familiar scent of the ocean.

The wooden deck felt sturdy and well-worn, a testament to the many gatherings that had taken place there over the years. Lin glanced around at the potted plants and flowers, all bathed in the soft glow of the overhead string lights before stepping to the edge of the deck near the patio.

"Queenie! Nicky!" she called out. In the distance, she could hear the faint rustle of the tall grass as her dog and Viv's cat began their trot back to the house.

Lin leaned on the railing, her thoughts drifting as she waited for the furry companions. She gazed out at the field where the tall grass swayed gently in the evening breeze.

"Hey there, you two," she said warmly as Nicky bounded onto the deck, his tail wagging furiously, followed by the more leisurely stride of Queenie. "Did you have fun exploring?"

Nicky barked happily, while Queenie merely

flicked her tail, sauntering past Lin with an air of feline indifference.

A sudden chill swept over her, causing a flood of unease to pulse in her chest. She turned to find the ghost of William Johnson standing beside her on the deck. His form flickered slightly as if struggling to stay present.

"William," Lin breathed, her heart pounding.

The ghost stared at the young woman and then extended a see-through hand toward her. As his fingers brushed close to Lin's forehead, a powerful vision flooded her mind.

The scene unfolded before her as if she were watching a movie ... the arsonist from 1901, his face obscured by shadows, stood with his back to her. He was dressed in old-fashioned clothing, and in his hand, he clutched a lit match. Moments later, the vision shifted, transforming into the modern-day arsonist — still seen only from the back — holding a bottle with a flaming rag stuffed into the top. The air was heavy with tension, and Lin could almost feel the heat of the flames as they licked at the arsonist's hand. The person started to turn toward her, but then the vision faded away.

Lin gripped the railing of the deck, her heart racing and her breath coming in short gasps. The image of the arsonist slipped through her fingers like smoke, leaving her with an unsettling sense of unease and urgency. She shook her head, trying to rid her thoughts of the lingering images and emotions that clouded her mind.

Lin glanced around for any sign of William, but he was gone, leaving her with questions and a sense of mounting dread.

Nicky and Queenie sat at her feet looking up at her.

"I'm okay." She rubbed her forehead. "Let's go inside." As Lin led them back into the kitchen and she closed the door behind her with a soft click, Jeff called to her. "Lin? Everything okay?"

"Y-yeah," she managed to stammer, still feeling disoriented. "I'm fine. I just ... had a vision."

Entering the cozy living room, Lin could see the curiosity and worry etched onto her relatives' faces. She took a deep breath, steeling herself for what she was about to share.

"I ... I saw something," she began hesitantly, her voice barely above a whisper. "William showed me a vision of the arsonist from 1901 ... and then he transformed into someone else, someone from our time. But I couldn't see his face, only his back."

"Was there any clue at all to who he was?" Viv

questioned. "Hair color? What he was wearing? A ring on his finger? Anything at all?"

"He was wearing a hoodie so I couldn't see his hair. I didn't notice anything else. It was over so fast."

As they all discussed potential leads, strategies, and ways to find the arsonist, Lin felt anxiety pulling at her.

"Did it look like Paul Hunter?" Viv asked softly.

"Maybe?" Lin shrugged. "Maybe not?"

"Listen," John began hesitantly, his gaze darting between Lin and the others, "we've been avoiding mentioning Brian's name, but we all know he could potentially help us with this. He's Paul's brother, after all."

"How could Brian help?" Jeff asked.

"Maybe," John said thoughtfully, "we could ask him about Paul's whereabouts during the fires, without directly accusing or implicating him."

"Wouldn't that be crossing a line?" Viv asked, concern etched on her face. "I mean, involving family in an investigation like this..."

Lin mulled over the implications. To involve Brian would be to betray a certain level of trust, yet they couldn't deny the potential benefits. "But if Brian finds out what we're really doing, it could damage our relationship with him. Not to mention, it might tip off Paul if he really is the arsonist."

While the group weighed the pros and cons of involving Brian, Lin's frustration grew. If only she could provide her vision as evidence, they wouldn't need to take such drastic measures.

"Ugh!" Lin exclaimed. "It's so frustrating knowing something but not being able to do anything about it."

Placing a hand on her shoulder, Jeff said gently, "We understand how you feel, but we have to work within the limitations of your abilities. And right now, that means finding concrete evidence to support your vision."

"Jeff's right," Viv chimed in. "We'll find a way to prove what you saw. It might take some time and effort, but we'll get there."

Lin took a deep breath. She knew they were right – they needed solid proof before accusing someone, but every moment they wasted felt like an opportunity for the arsonist to strike again.

"Okay," Lin finally conceded, forcing a smile. "We'll do this the hard way. Let's gather as much information as we can, but let's hold off on talking to Brian. I don't feel comfortable involving him in any of this."

With lives and homes at stake, Lin knew she might have to push aside her reservations about talking to Brian, but she hoped she wouldn't have to.

~

The next day in the late afternoon, Lin and Viv strolled through Nantucket's bustling downtown. The streets were alive with tourists and locals enjoying the warm weather and unique charm of the island.

"Lin, isn't that Michael Hansson over there?" Viv asked, nodding toward a lanky man chatting animatedly with a group of people outside a pub. Lin squinted against the sunlight, recognizing the firefighter they thought could be a suspect in the fires.

"Yeah, it's him," she replied, adjusting her grip on the bag of fresh produce they had just purchased at the farmers' market. "Let's go say hi."

As they approached, Michael's conversation with his friends seemed to wind down, the group dispersing with laughter and friendly pats on the back. Lin noticed that he held an empty beer bottle in one hand, and she studied it with interest.

"Hey, Michael," Viv called out, waving enthusiastically. "Nice day."

"Viv, Lin," Michael greeted them, a warm smile lighting up his face. "How are you two doing?"

"Can't complain," Lin replied, returning his smile. "Just enjoying this beautiful day. You, too?" She gestured to the beer bottle in his hand.

Michael laughed, a deep and hearty sound. "You could say that. A few other firefighters were just discussing the arson cases. The investigators might be on to a suspect, thanks to the specialty craft beer bottles used in the Molotov cocktails that started the blazes. And wouldn't you know it, I was drinking the very same brand."

"Really?" Viv's eyes widened, her curiosity piqued. "That's quite the coincidence."

"It sure is," Michael agreed, his expression turning serious for a moment. "I hope they catch the culprit soon. This island doesn't need that kind of trouble."

"We sure don't," Lin said under her breath, her thoughts racing.

"Anyway, I should get going," Michael said, brightening. "It was great to see you both. Take care."

"You too, Michael." Viv watched him as he set the beer bottle on a table and walked across the pub's patio.

As soon as he was out of earshot, Lin turned to

Viv, her eyes narrowed in thought. "Did you see what he was drinking?"

Viv's eyes widened in sudden realization. "It was Paul Hunter's new craft beer, Nantucket Seas."

"Exactly," Lin confirmed, her heart skipping a beat. "What if the arsonist really is Paul?"

Viv hesitated. "It would be horrible for that family. He'd be arrested and sent to prison. What would Beth and Brian do without him? It's too awful to even consider."

"From what Michael told us, the investigators might be ready to arrest someone."

"Michael's breath smelled heavily of beer," Viv said. "He really shouldn't have told us about the beer bottles being key to solving the crimes, not with an active investigation ongoing."

"You're right." Lin glanced at the empty beer bottle Michael had left on the table. "Maybe all of this will be over soon."

22

Beth stepped out onto the front porch, scanning the street for any sign of her younger brother. Brian had run off earlier that morning, overcome with grief on his first birthday without their mom. Beth couldn't blame him for being so upset, but she worried about him.

As the young woman walked down the driveway, she spotted two familiar faces across the street - Lin and Viv. The women smiled and waved when they saw her.

"Hey, Beth," Lin called out as she and Viv crossed over to the other side of the road. "Happy birthday to Brian. Is he around?"

Beth sighed, tucking a strand of hair behind her ear. "No, he's not. I was actually just about to go look for him. He's pretty torn up about it being his first birthday without Mom. She used to make him a special cupcake every year for his birthday," the young woman explained, her voice trembling slightly. "She'd bake a chocolate cupcake with strawberry frosting and put gold sprinkles all over the top. She'd put a single candle in it and she'd leave it on the breakfast table so Brian would see it first thing. It was their tradition."

Lin nodded. "But not this year," she said gently.

Beth swallowed hard, fighting back tears. "This year, there's no cupcake. With Mom and Dad passing away, it's just ... it's been so hard on all of us, especially Brian. He ran out of the house crying when he realized there wouldn't be a cupcake this year."

Viv shook her sympathetically. "Oh, that poor kid. I can't even imagine." She reached out and took Beth's hand reassuringly. "We'll help you find him. He can't have gone far."

"Really?" Beth perked up a bit. "That would be great, thanks."

"Of course," Lin said kindly. "Why don't we start by—"

Viv gently touched Lin's arm, interrupting her. "You know what, maybe we shouldn't rush into searching just yet. Brian probably needs a little time and space to process his emotions right now. It might be best to let Brian have some time to express his grief and calm himself down. There will be moments like this that will bring a loved one to mind, like a certain scent, a sound, hearing a piece of music, or seeing a book at the bookstore that the person loved – those things can bring up memories that hit hard and the grief flares up. I think your best bet is to stay home and wait for him, Beth. Give him a few hours to calm down, and if he's not back by then, we'll all go look together."

Beth considered this, absently twisting a strand of hair around her finger. "Yeah... you're probably right," she conceded after a moment. "I don't want to overwhelm him if he's not ready to talk yet. I'll give him some time to himself." She managed a small, grateful smile at Viv and Lin. "Thank you both. I appreciate your help."

Viv returned the smile warmly. "Let us know if you need anything else."

"Text us if he comes home," Lin told her.

With a wave, Beth turned and headed back up the driveway, hoping her little brother would come home soon.

"Before we head to get breakfast," Lin said to her cousin, "could we take a detour?" Since Lin didn't have to meet Leonard at a client's house for a couple of hours and Viv had plenty of coverage at the bookstore-café, the cousins had planned to get breakfast together that morning.

"Where do you want to go?" Viv eyed her companion with suspicion.

"I'd like to go to the cemetery again. I'd like to see Nathan Post's grave."

"Now? Why?" Viv asked as they walked along the sidewalk heading to a breakfast shop they liked.

"I just feel like I need to see it again."

Viv sighed. "I'm starving. I know if we go to the cemetery, it will end up being some long thing and I'll never get to eat."

With a chuckle, Lin told her, "It won't take long. I promise you'll get to eat. I'm hungry, too."

As they changed direction, Viv grumbled, pulling a granola bar from her small purse. "This will be my pathetic breakfast." She took a bite and said, "I have to admit I want to see that grave, too."

"You do?"

"Maybe seeing it will give us some insight into

who this arsonist is and we can take Paul Hunter off the suspect list."

"What about the Nantucket Seas beer bottles being used to make the Molotov cocktails?"

"Paul and his partner have sold some of the product. Other people have access to those bottles," Viv pointed out. "And what if someone is trying to frame Paul? Use his business's beer bottles to start fires and have the finger pointed at Paul for the crimes."

"I didn't think of that." Lin eyed Viv's granola bar. "Can I have a bite?"

Viv begrudgingly handed the bar to her cousin. "Let me remind you, we could have had a real breakfast."

Lin smiled. "But I'd rather share this with you."

They continued to the cemetery, the final resting place of some who had once called the island home, and they walked among the headstones.

"Here it is," Lin whispered as she stopped in front of a small, weathered headstone. The name and dates were barely legible, eroded by time and the salty sea air.

Viv stepped forward, her heart heavy with sorrow for the young life lost. She reached out, her fingertips touching the stone, and closed her eyes for a moment, offering a silent prayer for his poor soul. After a few moments, her eyes narrowed, "I know Nathan can't really be blamed for what he did. It was Arthur Radcliffe's fault. But why would someone ever resort to arson? It never ends well for anyone involved."

"Desperation, I guess," Lin suggested, her voice tinged with sadness. "Fear and anger can make people do terrible things." She looked around the cemetery, taking in the rows of graves that bore silent witness to countless lives and untold stories. "But it only causes more pain and suffering."

"Exactly," Viv agreed, her expression somber. "Think of all the families who've lost their homes, and one man was injured due to these fires. No one wins in a situation like this."

Lin nodded, her heart aching for all those affected by the recent string of arsons. She could feel the loss and helplessness that lingered in the air.

As they continued to contemplate the consequences of such actions, a sudden chill swept through the cemetery, despite the warm early June day. Lin shivered, feeling an unearthly presence nearby. She turned slowly, her gaze landing on the ghostly figure of William Johnson.

His ethereal form wavered slightly, as though

caught in a gentle breeze. His once fine clothes were now tattered and burned, a sad reminder of his fate. His eyes held a deep sorrow, fixated on the grave in front of them.

"William," Lin said softly, acknowledging his presence. "I know there's something about Nathan Post that's important to these recent fires. We're trying to figure out how he's connected to all of this."

William's spectral gaze shifted to Lin, gratitude evident in his eyes. He nodded solemnly, acknowledging her efforts to unravel the mystery behind the arsonist plaguing Nantucket.

"Can you help us understand?" Lin asked, her voice barely above a whisper. "We want to stop whoever is doing this before anyone else gets hurt."

William hesitated, his haunted eyes flickering between Lin and the worn headstone. It was as if he wanted to speak but couldn't find the words. Lin's heart ached for the ghost, understanding that even in death, the tragedy still haunted him.

"We want to help. We need your guidance."

The ghostly figure seemed to gather his strength, determination showing on his face. He slowly reached out his hand, pointing toward the grave of Nathan Post.

Lin and Viv stood rooted to the spot with Lin

watching William Johnson's ghostly form glide toward Nathan Post's grave. The ethereal figure seemed to shimmer in the morning light. Suddenly, sparkling atoms swirled in the air and a new ghost appeared standing next to William. Lin was startled to see a boy of about fifteen staring back at her.

"Look," Lin whispered to Viv, her voice hushed with wonder. "It's the ghost of Nathan Post. William is putting his arm around Nathan."

Viv squinted. "Is he ... comforting the boy?"

"It seems so," Lin murmured, her surprise evident. She had not expected such a kind and tender gesture from William toward someone who had caused him so much pain. Yet, there they were – two ghosts bound by tragedy and forgiveness, seeking solace in each other.

"Unbelievable," she thought aloud, her heart swelling. Perhaps even in death, redemption was possible. "William is showing kindness to Nathan, despite everything he did."

As Lin continued to observe the scene, she noticed something strange happening. Nathan's face began to blur and fade as if being erased from existence. And then, just as suddenly, Brian Hunter's face appeared in its place, looking lost and afraid.

The Haunted Fire

"Viv!" Lin exclaimed, gripping her cousin's arm tightly. "Did you see that? It was Brian's face!"

"See what?" Viv asked, concern lacing her words. "What happened?"

"Brian's face replaced Nathan's for a moment, before it returned to normal," Lin explained, her voice shaking. "The arsonist isn't Paul. It's Brian. This is a message from William, a warning to stop Brian from ending up like Nathan, trapped in guilt, sorrow, and regret," she explained, her mind racing as she pieced together the puzzle. "He wants us to stop Brian before it's too late."

"Oh, my gosh," Viv gasped, finally understanding the gravity of the situation. "We need to find Brian."

Lin's eyes never left the spot where William and Nathan's ghosts stood. She knew that they had been given a rare and precious opportunity – a chance to change the course of events, to prevent history from repeating itself. "Let's go," she whispered.

Together, the cousins turned away from the cemetery. They had to find Brian Hunter and save him from himself, ensuring that the tragic legacy of Nathan Post would not be carried into the future. The ghosts had shown them the way, and now it was up to them to see it through.

23

After Lin and Viv finished their workdays early, the cousins walked down the sidewalks of Nantucket looking for Brian when suddenly Viv's phone buzzed to life. She glanced at the screen and her rosy cheeks lost some of their color. "It's Beth," she said before answering the call.

"Hey, Beth, what's up?" Viv asked lightly, though her muscles tensed up with worry.

Lin could hear the faint sound of Beth's panicked words on the other end of the line.

"Slow down, Beth. What's going on?" Viv held her breath, waiting for the young woman's response. Lin watched her cousin's eyes widen, and she felt a knot tightening in her stomach.

"Wait ... the police are at your house? They're

questioning Paul about the fires?" Viv's voice cracked slightly.

Lin's heart raced. *It's not Paul. It's Brian. He's the arsonist.* But they had no way to prove it yet.

"Listen, Beth, I know this is scary, but I promise you, everything will be okay," Viv said, gripping the phone tightly. Her gold-flecked hair framed her face as she focused intently on comforting her friend. "Paul has nothing to hide," she said firmly, hoping she sounded more confident than she felt. Guilt gnawed at her for not being fully honest with Beth, but she couldn't reveal their suspicions about Brian just yet. "Just make sure Paul tells the truth, and the investigators will see he's innocent."

Lin squeezed Viv's free hand, offering silent support. She wished there was more she could do.

Viv said hesitantly, "Have you heard from Brian? Has he come back to the house yet? Do you know where he is?"

There was a pause on the other end of the line before Beth's voice came through, tinged with worry. "No, I haven't seen him since this morning. He hasn't come back. I hope he's okay. I called him a few times, but he won't answer. I was about to go out looking for him when the investigators arrived."

"We're just leaving town right now. We'll keep an

eye out for him. If we don't see him, we'll wander around the neighborhoods and see if we can find him. Take care of yourself and Paul."

As Viv hung up the phone, Lin's eyes narrowed. The weight of the situation bore down on them, pressing against their chests like the humidity of a hot early June day.

Lin and Viv exchanged worried glances. Their walk through town had taken a dark turn, leaving them both with a growing sense of dread. They needed to find Brian, and they needed to find him soon – before more lives were put in danger.

"I was sure he would have gone home by now. We need to find him," Lin stated. "This is getting out of hand. I feel really anxious. Something's going to happen. We should have looked for him right after we left the cemetery."

Viv nodded, her rosy cheeks paling at the thought of another fire ravaging a home.

"Should we split up and search?" Viv asked, her voice trembling slightly.

Lin glanced around the streets, her heart pounding a drumbeat in her ears. "I'd rather stay together."

As the two cousins set off, their minds racing with worst-case scenarios, each one had the feeling that time was running out. Would they find Brian in time to stop another fire?

Searching through the town for any sign of Brian, a chill sent a shudder down Lin's spine. She knew that another fire could be sparked at any moment. "Let's head to the neighborhoods around the Quaker cemetery," she suggested, and the two headed in that direction. Shadows gathered as the sun slipped lower in the sky.

"Do you smell something?" Viv sniffed the air.

"Oh, no." Lin's heart sank.

Hurrying through the small streets and lanes, Lin caught sight of it – an ominous orange glow coming from behind a row of homes. Her heart skipped a beat, dread tightening its icy grip around her throat.

"Viv! It's another fire! On the next street over. I can see the top of the house," Lin told her cousin.

They could see smoke billowing out from the roof of the house so they broke into a run and rushed around the corner to see people gathering in front of the home. As they approached the burning building, their eyes watered from the acrid smoke billowing from the blazing structure. The once-charming home was now engulfed in flames.

"Is anyone inside?" Lin asked a bystander who

stood watching the destruction, his face illuminated by the dancing firelight.

"Pauline Lancaster lives here," he replied, his voice shaking. "She's in her early nineties. Her caretaker has the day off. She's in there all alone."

Lin cursed under her breath, scanning the house for any sign of movement within. She couldn't just stand by and do nothing – not when someone's life was at stake. *Brian set this fire*, she thought. *If Pauline dies....*

"Viv, I'm going in. When the fire department arrives, tell them Pauline and I are inside." Lin's voice wavered, but she forced herself to stay strong.

"Lin, wait for me!" Viv pleaded, but Lin was already making her way toward the house.

"You stay out here. Pauline needs help now," Lin shouted to her cousin, steeling herself for what she was about to do. "I'll be careful, I promise."

"Lin, no. Don't go in there." Viv's eyes filled with tears.

Ignoring her cousin's pleas, she asked a bystander if they knew the layout of the house and if they could tell her where Pauline might be.

"Yes, I've been inside many times." A woman in her sixties described the first floor layout, her voice strained with urgency. "Pauline's bedroom is on the first floor at the back of the house. She spends most of her time in her room."

"Thank you," Lin whispered. Running as fast as she could, she disappeared around the corner of the burning house, determined to save Pauline Lancaster from the arsonist's flames.

Smoke billowed around her as she approached the back entrance, the heat nearly singeing her skin even through her clothes. She pulled her shirt up to cover her nose and mouth like a mask in hopes of filtering the smoke and then pushed open the back door, stepping into the hellish landscape. The fire reflected in Lin's wide eyes as she took in the nightmarish scene.

"Pauline!" Lin choked out between coughs as she stumbled forward, her eyes watering from the smoke. She knew time was running out, but she couldn't afford to panic. Not now, not when someone's life was in danger.

"I'm here," Pauline's weak voice called out, barely audible over the crackling fire.

"I'm coming!" Lin shouted, relief surging through her at the sound of the elderly woman's voice. Following the sound, she moved deeper into the house, the thick smoke obscuring her vision as she felt along the walls trying to find the doorway to the primary bedroom.

Then, through the gloom, she spotted an open door. The bedroom! Lin dropped to her hands and knees, crawling below the worst of the smoke.

The room was sweltering, the air heavy with smoke, but there she was – Pauline Lancaster, frail and trembling, curled up on the floor beside her bed.

Tears streamed down Pauline's soot-streaked face. "I ... tried to get out ... but I can't ... my legs..." she choked out the words between coughs.

"Save your strength," Lin said, trying to sound calm and confident despite her own fear. She bent down and carefully helped Pauline to her feet; the elderly woman's frail body weighed next to nothing.

"Okay, Pauline, we're getting out of here," Lin whispered, determination burning within her as fiercely as the flames that surrounded them. "Just hold on tight." Her words were punctuated by bouts of coughing as she tried to navigate the smoke-filled house while holding tight to Pauline's arm. Each breath practically seared her lungs. Sweat poured down her face. The smoke was so thick she could barely see a foot in front of her.

"I can't see the way out," Lin groaned, reaching

up to touch her horseshoe necklace for a moment. *Help us get out of here*, she implored her ancestors.

Outside, with Viv praying for the fire trucks to arrive, Brian Hunter, wide-eyed and panting, arrived at the scene. His gaze went immediately to the roaring flames that engulfed Pauline Lancaster's home.

"Brian!" Viv called out, grabbing his arm and pulling him close so he could hear her over the noise. "Pauline is still inside! Lin went in to save her. I'm afraid they won't come out."

"Wh – What?" Brian stammered, fear clawing at his heart. He had never intended for this. He thought the house was empty. "I – I have to help them!"

"Brian, wait!" Viv shouted after him, but it was too late – Brian had already dashed headlong toward the inferno, his guilt spurring him forward like he was possessed.

"Pauline ... talk to me. Keep talking..." Lin urged the elderly woman, her voice hoarse from the smoke. She knew that staying conscious and focused would be their key to survival.

"You're so strong. We'll get out," Pauline whispered, her voice barely audible above the roar of the fire.

Lin felt her strength waning, the smoke and heat sapping away her energy, and for a moment, she thought she could see her ancestors, Emily and Sebastian Coffin standing in the smoke a few yards away from her. She reached her hand to them.

"Lin! Pauline!" Brian's voice echoed faintly through the dense smoke as he ventured deeper into the burning house.

"Here," Lin croaked, her throat raw from the smoke. "We're in the hall."

"Stay where you are!" Brian yelled back, determination driving him forward. "I'm almost there!"

"Please hurry..." Lin whispered, her vision blurring as she struggled to maintain consciousness. She had to stay awake ... she had to stay awake.

"Lin!" The sound of Brian's voice grew closer.

Lin blinked her eyes, trying to clear the haze from her vision as Brian's figure emerged from the thick smoke.

"Brian..." Lin breathed a sigh of relief, even as the fire continued its relentless assault on the house.

"Come on, there's a way out," Brian said urgently, his face streaked with soot. He bent down and effortlessly scooped Pauline into his arms, nodding for Lin to follow him.

"Lead the way," Lin rasped, mustering the last of

her strength to keep up with Brian's long strides. The trio moved quickly through the fiery inferno, as Brian navigated the smoke-filled maze.

"Almost there..." Brian said under his breath, anxiety furrowing his brow despite his best efforts at maintaining control. As they rounded a corner, a wall of flames erupted, blocking their path; but without missing a beat, Brian kicked open a door to reveal a staircase leading to the basement.

"Down here," he instructed, carefully descending the steps with Pauline cradled protectively in his arms. Lin followed closely behind, her legs trembling with exhaustion. Brian led the way through the dark basement, their footsteps echoing off concrete walls as they raced toward the dim light filtering through the windows of a door.

"Get Pauline out," Lin insisted as they reached the door, her body trembling from both fear and exhaustion.

Brian pushed the door open and carefully carried Pauline through the opening. A man's hands appeared on the other side, pulling Pauline to safety. The woman's eyes fluttered open and she coughed weakly, but she was alive. They'd made it out.

"Let's get out of here," Brian said, grabbing Lin's hand and pulling her outside. Lin felt a surge of gratitude for the young man who had risked his life to save them. She stumbled onto the grass and almost fell, but Brian caught her arm and steadied her.

"Thank you, Brian," she whispered, her voice choked with emotion. Her legs were shaky and her throat was raw from the smoke, but the fresh air was already reviving her.

In the distance, sirens wailed as more emergency vehicles raced toward them. The fire raged on inside the house, flames licking out of the broken windows. They'd gotten out just in time. Lin looked over at Pauline, who was sitting up now, dazed but unharmed. A pair of paramedics hurried over with oxygen masks and blankets for the woman.

Brian gazed at the burning building, his face etched with terrible shame, sorrow, and guilt. "I did this."

"I know," Lin told him softly.

"I never meant for this to happen," he said quietly. "I didn't think anyone was at home."

Lin put a hand on his shoulder. "I know, but we have to tell the truth now. To the police, and to Paul and Beth."

Brian took a deep breath and nodded, tears rolling down his cheeks.

The young man had set the fire, but Lin could

see his remorse, and he'd risked his own life coming into the burning building to save her and Pauline Lancaster.

Firefighters led Brian and Lin to the front of the house, and when Viv saw her cousin, she rushed forward across the lawn and wrapped Lin in her arms.

"That was a stupid, stupid thing to do. Don't ever do that again," Viv cried with tears streaming down her face as she hugged her cousin. "You almost gave me a heart attack. I swear I could kill you." Viv looked up and down at her cousin. "Are you all right? You're not hurt, are you?"

Catching her breath and watching the flames devour the house, Lin smiled as her own tears tumbled from her eyes. "I'm fine ... now that I'm out here with you."

24

The sun glinted off the rippling blue waves as Lin closed her eyes, feeling the gentle sea breeze caress her face. She took a deep breath, inhaling the fresh salty air.

"Ahoy there, landlubbers!" John called out from behind the wheel. "Who's ready for an adventure?"

Lin opened her eyes to see Nicky already perched eagerly on the bow of John's boat, tail wagging. She laughed. "I think you've got at least one volunteer, Captain."

John grinned and called the dog off the bow. "Go stand with Lin, Nick. I don't want you falling overboard."

The dog left the bow as John pushed the throttle

forward, and the boat leapt over the swells, salt spray mingling with the wind.

Lin whooped, the speed and power exhilarating. Beside her, Jeff cheered and laughed.

After a few minutes, John eased back on the gas and swung the boat in a wide arc. The island came into better view, its trees and white-sand beaches glowing emerald and ivory in the sun.

The ocean breeze blew Lin's hair around as she gazed out over the sparkling blue water. Beside her on the boat, Viv chatted happily with Jeff about her latest exploits in the bookshop while John expertly steered them along the coast.

Nicky's ears perked up and he gave a cheerful bark as a seagull circled overhead.

"It's so peaceful out here," Lin said, closing her eyes for a moment to fully absorb the sun's warmth.

"Sure is. I'm glad we could all take the day to enjoy it," John replied.

Lin nodded. After the stress of the arson investigation, she was grateful for this chance to relax with her family.

When Queenie gave a sleepy meow from her spot curled up on a blanket, Viv laughed and scratched the cat behind her ears.

Jeff put an arm around Lin's shoulders. "Hard to

believe all the craziness we've been through lately. Feels good to just be out here with no worries, doesn't it?"

"It sure does," Lin agreed.

"Who's up for a swim?" John called out, maneuvering the boat closer to shore.

"I'm in!" Viv said, kicking off her sandals and slipping off her coverup to reveal a purple one-piece swimsuit. She jumped in after Jeff, creating a splash.

Laughing, Lin was next, jumping into the cool water moments before John cannonballed into the sea.

"This feels amazing," Lin said, floating on her back and gazing up at the clouds drifting by.

Laughter filled the air as they horsed around in the water for a while, splashing each other playfully. Having no interest in getting wet, Queenie watched them from the boat comfortably resting on a deck chair in the shade.

"Come on, Nicky!" Lin called out, encouraging their dog to join them in the water. Instead, the small mixed breed happily jumped onto a paddle board, tail wagging as he watched his human family frolicking in the waves.

Nicky barked excitedly, balancing on the paddleboard as Jeff pushed him around in the water. The little dog's tail wagged furiously when Lin swam over to give him a pat.

"Last one to the old buoy is a rotten egg!" Viv challenged, her eyes twinkling with mischief.

"You're on!" John replied with a grin, and soon enough, the four of them were racing toward the floating marker in the distance.

Lin swam with strong, determined strokes, feeling the muscles in her arms and legs propel her forward. She smiled hearing the friendly banter between her family members, their laughter echoing across the water.

Eventually, as they made their way back to the boat, breathless and refreshed, John said, "I don't know about you three, but I've worked up an appetite."

They climbed back aboard and wrapped up in towels.

After their swim, Jeff got to work on dinner, grilling up cheeseburgers and veggie kabobs as the sun sank lower in the sky. They sat together around the table on the deck, watching the sunset paint the horizon in hues of orange, pink, and violet.

"Mmm, this potato salad is delicious," Lin said. "Great idea to picnic on the boat today."

Viv nodded; her mouth full.

Between bites, they chatted and laughed, simply enjoying the food and company. Overhead, seagulls cried as they circled, hoping for scraps.

"Can you believe the arson case is finally over?" Viv asked, taking a bite of her burger.

Lin shook her head. "We were pretty sure it was Paul, until the last day or so. It's hard to believe a fifteen-year-old would do something so dangerous, but he's completely grief-stricken over losing his parents."

"The poor kid," Jeff chimed in. "It's too much emotional trauma. It's not an excuse for what he did, but it's a reason."

John whistled softly. "Paul must feel awful, knowing his bottles were used for something so destructive."

Jeff sighed. "I spoke to Paul earlier. He's devastated. He blames himself for not seeing Brian's pain more clearly."

"The police thought Paul was the arsonist at first since Brian used his brother's craft beer bottles for the Molotov cocktails," Viv added.

Lin nodded. "This will haunt their family for a long time. Brian's looking at some serious consequences. Someone could've been killed." She shivered, remembering the searing heat from the flames at Pauline's house. If it hadn't been for Brian rushing in to help her, things would have ended very differently.

"At least now the ghost can rest," Lin said. "His unfinished business was ensuring the same fate didn't happen to Brian as it did to Nathan Post back in 1901."

The others murmured agreement.

Lin's thoughts were interrupted by Viv. "I hope Paul and Beth will be okay. They seem so dedicated to getting Brian help."

Jeff nodded. "Paul and Beth have started counseling to help them deal with everything."

"What kind of punishment is Brian facing?" John asked.

Viv sighed. "From what Lin and I have heard, up to six months in juvenile detention, several years of probation, community service, restitution for damages, and a hefty fine."

"That's a lot for a teen to take on," Jeff said.

"At least he'll have Paul and Beth's support. I can't imagine how difficult this must be for them, too, trying to help their brother while dealing with their own grief and shock," Lin added. "Brian will have to deal with the stigma of being an arsonist for a long while, but he can build a good life for himself and go on to do good things."

With stomachs full, they leaned back in their seats, gazing out at the shimmering water and basking in the warmth of the evening. Silence settled over the group as the sun dipped below the horizon with each of them contemplating the ripple effects from Brian's actions - how many lives had been changed by the events of the past weeks.

∽

Lin reflected on the ghost's intentions as she, Jeff, and Nicky walked up to their house after a long day out on John's boat. She now clearly understood that the ghost simply wanted to prevent Brian from suffering the same fate as the troubled boy from 1901.

Wandering over to the back deck, she leaned on the railing and looked out at the riot of climbing roses and hydrangeas she had planted.

Lin thought about how much Brian reminded her of the ghost boy — angry, sad, desperate. But there was still hope for Brian. With the right help, he would still have a future, unlike the boy whose bones lay buried in the nearby cemetery.

The past could not be changed, but the present was theirs to shape. Lin smiled softly, breathing in the sweet scent of the flowers in their garden.

She closed her eyes, letting the peace of the evening soak in. Suddenly, she could feel the ghosts' presence — a gentle tingling like static electricity raised the hairs on her arms.

When she turned around, two shimmering forms stood before her on the deck. The ghosts of William and Nathan watched her. Their outlines were hazy in the fading light, but she could see their faces clearly. They were smiling; their eyes shining.

Lin's breath caught in her throat. "I hope you feel at peace now," she whispered.

The ghosts nodded, still smiling, then, in unison, they brought their transparent hands up and placed them over the spots where their hearts would be.

Lin's vision blurred with tears. "I understand," she said softly. "Your work is done. You can rest now."

The ghosts flickered, their edges starting to dissolve into particles of light.

"Thank you," Lin said, her voice thick with emotion, "for trusting me. For letting me help."

The ghosts' smiles glowed brighter, lighting up the deepening twilight, and then the particles flashed and swirled, enveloping the deck in a warm, dazzling glow.

When the light faded, the ghosts were gone. Lin let out a long, slow breath as the goosebumps on her arms settled down. A deep sense of peace filled her heart.

It was over. The ghosts had moved on. The living had been saved, and she knew she would carry this moment with her always.

Taking a moment to collect herself, she wiped tears from her eyes as she gazed out at the field. She knew she should head inside but couldn't bring herself to move just yet.

The events of the past few weeks replayed in her mind — the fires, the fear, the unraveling mystery. She thought of young Brian, nearly destroyed by grief, but she had hope for his future.

Mostly though, her thoughts lingered on Nathan and William. She wished she could have learned more about who they were when they were alive, but the important thing was that they were at peace now. Their souls were free.

Finally, Lin turned and headed inside where she was greeted by the warm glow of lamps in the kitchen and the smell of something delicious baking in the oven.

Jeff smiled. "Hey. I was starting to think you fell asleep out there. Our dessert is just about ready. Everything okay?"

With a contented sigh, Lin smiled and gave him a kiss on the cheek. "Yes, I'm fine."

After everything that had happened, an evening of tea, something sweet, and her husband's company was just what she needed.

"The ghosts were here. They came to say goodbye."

Jeff gently touched her cheek. "You helped them ... and Brian. They're lucky to have you, just like I am."

She wrapped her husband in a loving embrace. The ghosts had departed, and all was right with the world.

At least, until the next ghost showed up.

THANK YOU FOR READING!

Books by J.A. Whiting can be found here:
www.amazon.com/author/jawhiting

To hear about new books and book sales, please sign up for our mailing list at:
www.jawhiting.com

Your email will never be sold, shared, or spammed.

If you enjoyed the book, please consider leaving a review. A few words are all that's needed. It would be very much appreciated.

BOOKS BY J. A. WHITING

SWEET COVE PARANORMAL COZY MYSTERIES

LIN COFFIN PARANORMAL COZY MYSTERIES

CLAIRE ROLLINS PARANORMAL COZY MYSTERIES

MURDER POSSE PARANORMAL COZY MYSTERIES

PAXTON PARK PARANORMAL COZY MYSTERIES

ELLA DANIELS WITCH COZY MYSTERIES

SEEING COLORS PARANORMAL COZY MYSTERIES

OLIVIA MILLER MYSTERIES (not cozy)

SWEET ROMANCES by JENA WINTER

COZY BOX SETS

BOOKS BY J.A. WHITING & NELL MCCARTHY

HOPE HERRING PARANORMAL COZY MYSTERIES

TIPPERARY CARRIAGE COMPANY COZY MYSTERIES

BOOKS BY J.A. WHITING & ARIEL SLICK

GOOD HARBOR WITCHES PARANORMAL COZY MYSTERIES

BOOKS BY J.A. WHITING & AMANDA DIAMOND

PEACHTREE POINT COZY MYSTERIES

DIGGING UP SECRETS PARANORMAL COZY MYSTERIES

BOOKS BY J.A. WHITING & MAY STENMARK

MAGICAL SLEUTH PARANORMAL WOMEN'S FICTION COZY MYSTERIES

HALF MOON PARANORMAL MYSTERIES

VISIT US

jawhiting.com

bookbub.com/authors/j-a-whiting

amazon.com/author/jawhiting

facebook.com/jawhitingauthor

bingebooks.com/author/ja-whiting

J A WHITING
Books and More

Printed in Great Britain
by Amazon